WHITE DEATH

JACK CASTLE

EDGE SCIENCE FICTION AND FANTASY PUBLISHING
An Imprint of HADES PUBLICATIONS, INC.
CALGARY

White Death

EDGE SCIENCE FICTION AND FANTASY PUBLISHING
An Imprint of HADES PUBLICATIONS, INC.
P.O. Box 1714, Calgary, Alberta, T2P 2L7, Canada

The EDGE Team:
Producer: Brian Hades
Acquisitions Editor: Ella Beaumont
Edited by: Christine Mains
Cover Design: Ella Beaumont
Cover Art Elements: 123RF Stock Photo, salman2, kanzefar, kikujungboy, afhunta, williamlangeveld
Book Design: Mark Steele
Publicist: Janice Shoults

ISBN: 978-1-77053-134-5

EDGE Science Fiction and Fantasy Publishing and Hades Publications, Inc. acknowledges the ongoing support of the Alberta Foundation for the Arts and the Canada Council for the Arts for our publishing programme.

Canada Council   Conseil des arts
for the Arts   du Canada

Library and Archives Canada Cataloguing in Publication
CIP Data on file with the National Library of Canada
ISBN: 978-1-77053-134-5
(e-Book ISBN: 978-1-77053-133-8)

FIRST EDITION
(20161108)
Printed in USA
www.edgewebsite.com

Publisher's Note:

Thank you for purchasing this book. It began as an idea, was shaped by the creativity of its talented author, and was subsequently molded into the book you have before you by a team of editors and designers.

Like all EDGE books, this book is the result of the creative talents of a dedicated team of individuals who all believe that books (whether in print or pixels) have the magical ability to take you on an adventure to new and wondrous places powered by the author's imagination.

As EDGE's publisher, I hope that you enjoy this book. It is a part of our ongoing quest to discover talented authors and to make their creative writing available to you.

We also hope that you will share your discovery and enjoyment of this novel on social media through Facebook, Twitter, Goodreads, Pinterest, etc., and by posting your opinions and/or reviews on Amazon and other review sites and blogs. By doing so, others will be able to share your discovery and passion for this book.

Brian Hades, publisher

Dedications

Dedicated to those who kept the dream alive:
My Wife Tracy
My two best friends, Chad Bryant and Greg Wahlman
My Mentor, Dr. J.P. Waller
And my newest pal, Ryan Chidester
Our Lord and Savior.

A special dedication goes out to my former patrol Sergeant at Anchorage Police Department, Sgt. Dennis Allen. Thank you Denny for fact-checking this book, your military service, (Major in the Air Force, (Ret) and recipient of the Distinguished Flying Cross), and all of your years serving in law enforcement. You are a true hero my friend.
The world is a better place for you having been in it.

I would also like to acknowledge and thank the fine folks at EDGE Science Fiction and Fantasy Publishing: Acquisitions Editor Ella Beaumont (and rollercoaster junkie), Editor Supreme Christine Mains, Publicist (and Fairy God-Mamma) Janice Shoults, Formatter and Super-Support Man Mark Steele, and of course, the Mad Hatter in charge of it all, Mr. Brian Hades.

Facts

The Arctic Ice Cap covers an area twice as big as the United States, but is melting at a rate of 200 feet per day, exposing landmass and artifacts that have not seen the light of day for over 10,000 years.

The Arctic has been called the last unexplored territory, and by others, The Atlantis of the North.

Since 2008, commercial ships have already begun sojourning across this long searched for North West passage.

In 2009 a Russian Submarine planted a flag at the bottom of the Arctic Ocean laying claim to untold riches of oil, minerals, and fisheries. As a result, an Arctic nation council was formed and land rites have been disputed over ever since.

Expert futurologists predict by 2025 coastal cities, ports, tour ships, shipping lanes, and drilling platforms will be as commonplace in the Arctic as they are in every other coastal waterway in the world.

In 2002, Marine Archeologists discovered a vast undersea city, (Five miles long and Two miles wide) off the coast of India. Carbon dating of recovered artifacts date the city to be at least 9,500 years old, (that's 5,000 years older than the oldest known civilization in recorded history!). They believe this city, along with many others, was submerged during the last ice age.

Last year, off the northern coast of Alaska, (at a depth of 150 feet), a team of Chinese Geologists studying tectonic plates in their submersible stumbled across a solid Jade stone marker on the Alaskan ice shelf. The survey team also photographed remnants of a city with massive walls and plazas scattered across a large area of seabed. When Marine Archeologists returned to the coordinates, despite their best efforts, they were unable to locate the jade totem or the underwater city ever again.

WHITE DEATH

Prologue

"Iditarod Dad"

Unless you're the lead dog, the view never changes. *Har-har-har.*

These were the thoughts of Tom Holden as he stared at the rumps of his dog sled team. He was running the Iditarod Trail Sled Dog Race in Alaska, traveling through 1,149 miles of the most rugged and cruel landscape of the Last Frontier … and he was in last place.

Holden had never had any illusions about winning. In fact, it surprised him he had made it this far over the harsh tundra, through the jagged mountain passes, and across deadly rivers of ice. He wasn't a professional musher, not by a long shot. In fact, the only reason he was running this ridiculous test of endurance was the locket hanging around his neck. Inside was a picture of his beautiful nineteen-year-old daughter, Shannon. The picture had been taken before the spinal meningitis did its job and she wasted away before his eyes. These were Shannon's dogs, not his. Shannon had raised them from pups and trained them. Her dying wish had been that he run her dogs in the Iditarod race. She told him he didn't have to win or anything. "Just run 'em, dad, run 'em for me." Now, he wasn't a musher, but he had helped Shannon train her dogs enough to know what he was doing, and he was damned if he was going to let his little girl down, even if it killed him.

Like every year, print and television journalists, along with crowds of spectators, attended the various checkpoints along the trail. Somehow, word had gotten out about why he was running the race, and the reporters swelled in number at each checkpoint. At the Skwentna checkpoint, it had been the worst. Three-time Iditarod champions were rudely ignored when he had finally sledded into town. It seemed the world couldn't get enough of a father trying to fulfill his daughter's dying wish. At least the press had put a nice photo of Shannon in the paper. That had made Shannon's mother happy, which she hadn't been for some time.

The trail from the ceremonial start in Anchorage had started out easy enough, sledding over low flat lowlands, and well marked by flags and reflectors. But from there the trail had gotten pretty tough, so much so that mushers started dropping out of the race at a rate of about one every seventy-five miles.

The race had started with forty-two mushers, each with approximately sixteen dogs, but one musher broke her hand right outside of Willow, and another had three of his dogs trampled by a charging moose in "Moose Alley." Another nine teams had dropped out in a fierce blizzard that had struck them in McGrath. That storm had caused whiteout conditions and sub-zero temperatures. Plus, the gale force winds had erased all the trail markers, making the path hard to follow, but Shannon had programed his GPS, and he had weathered the storm just fine. Shannon had also made sure her dad had all the right gear: food, spare dog booties, headlamps, tools, sled parts for repairs, and spare batteries for his night headlamp, and even a satellite phone. They had made the final preparations for his trip in her hospital room, spreading out maps on the foot of her bed. Shannon had made him study the route as carefully as he had scrutinized maps on missions in Afghanistan as a younger man over twenty years before. The trip planning had become a welcome relief from the constant reminder of her imminent departure.

Holden took small comfort in the fact that he was past the worst stretch of the trail, the Dalzell Gorge, a divide that drops one thousand feet in elevation in five miles. Holden had had to ride the brake most of the way down and sometimes use his snow hook for traction. At the bottom of the gorge, one musher had fallen through an ice bridge and had to be airlifted out, bringing the total mushers left in the race to just thirty. But all of them were more experienced than Holden, so if by some miracle Holden did finish, he knew he was a shoe in for the Red Lantern award.

The banks of the trail were lined with snow-covered alders; quarter-sized snowflakes fell from the sky. For most, the wilderness was inspiring, but Holden felt this portion of the trail was long miles of vast emptiness, and his tired muscles ached for a couple of hours of bunking down at the next checkpoint.

After what seemed like an eternity, the narrow corridor through the woods finally began to widen. As the trees became sparser, Holden could make out a huge bonfire in the town up ahead. He knew from Shannon's meticulous tutorial that the next checkpoint would be the ghost town of Takotna, a real commercial hub during Alaska's gold rush days but now, with the exception of Iditarod week, practically a ghost town.

Already he was dreading the host of reporters that would be there to greet him. All he wanted to do was feed his dogs and lie down for some rest, but he'd talk to the reporters for Shannon's sake, and for her mother's.

The bonfire seemed bigger than the others, but as the trail broadened into an open field before him, Holden realized ... it wasn't a bonfire that was burning.

It was the town. —— <> ——

Holden pulled on the reins, kicked the brake, and brought his team to a stop. He dropped his snow hook for good measure and dismounted the sled in disbelief.

He yanked off his snow mitts and dropped them on the sled, a decision he would come to regret later. As he raised his goggles onto his forehead, he noted that not all the buildings were on fire. The big buildings on the corners were ablaze, but thus far the remainder of the abandoned town was still unscathed. And thanks to the wet snow, the fires were steadily dying out on their own with minimal risk of spreading.

Where the hell is everybody?

The place should've been swarming with reporters, mushers, and invaluable support personnel. Now, there wasn't a soul to be found. Before venturing deeper into the old town, he noted the dogs were sniffing the air as though their noses were detecting something unfamiliar. Normally, they would be barking with excitement and pulling at their tethers to be free. It was these kinds of observations that had kept him and his squad alive overseas.

Holden began searching the old buildings and saw dropped belongings: backpacks, cameras, clothes, all lying in the middle of the street, where the reporters and spectators must have dropped them. Passing the burning buildings, he approached the tiny Main Street located between two rows of dilapidated buildings. Immediately apparent was a large orange Buick in the middle of the street. The left blinker was flashing and the door was wide open. He could hear the engine still chugging and see vapor puffing out the tailpipe. Whatever had happened here, it couldn't have been more than a couple of hours ago.

As he rounded the Buick's trunk, he glanced down and noticed red stains on the snow. The streaks of blood originated from the open car door. They scratched across the powdery snow in the direction of one of the dilapidated buildings, a rickety wooden structure labeled HARDWARE STORE, only most of the letters were partially illegible from neglect. The funny thing was that the blood trails didn't go inside the slanted broken doorway but up the sides of the wallboards and up onto the tin roof. Holden had hiked through the woods enough to know bears were more than capable of climbing trees, but could they climb up the side of walls?

It was common for mushers to suffer from sleep deprivation and to experience hallucinations, but Holden had survived Ranger school, one of the toughest combat courses in the world. Even though that had been twenty years ago, and the Iditarod had been grueling, he didn't think he was seeing things now.

Although rare, it wasn't unheard of for a hibernating bear to wake up hungry during winter because it hadn't stored up enough fat in the fall, but what kind of bear could drag a human being up the side of a building? Holden decided he didn't want to find out. He suddenly became painfully aware that he had left his satellite phone and his own little addition to the expedition, a Taurus Model 44, back on the dogsled.

Damn, rookie mistake. Former Ranger, my butt.

He spun on his heel to trek back to his sled to retrieve both weapon and phone when he heard a woman cry out, "Please help me!" The voice was followed by a desperate shriek that came from inside the hardware store.

Staggering out of the darkness of the slanted doorway was a young woman who couldn't have been much older than Shannon. Half the woman's clothes had been torn away, and she was missing one boot. Her hand was outstretched towards him while the other held onto her stomach. Holden had seen enough combat wounds to recognize the squishy blue tentacles leaking out of her abdomen. Something had eviscerated this poor girl and left her to die.

"Oh, thank God, please help me!" she cried, taking two steps towards him.

Every fiber in his being told him to run for the phone and gun, but he also knew he could never leave this young girl behind to die.

Hesitating only seconds, he started towards her. She managed another step before falling to her knees and then collapsing onto her face.

When he reached her, Holden dropped down onto his knees beside her. "Don't worry. I've got you. You're going to be okay." It was a lie, but he had to say something.

The young woman lost consciousness. Realizing that time was a luxury he did not have, he quickly began removing the small first aid kit he kept on his belt. But in the few seconds it took him to turn away to unzip the kit, something in the hardware store reached out of the shadows, grabbed the young woman by her ankles, and dragged her back inside with such tremendous force that Holden fell backwards.

"Holy crap!" He hadn't seen what had snatched the young woman. It had happened in seconds. He contemplated going into the darkened interior after her, but then he heard a loud rumble emanating deep within the chest of something very large and very pissed off.

The girl must've woken up because Holden heard a loud scream within. This was cut off almost immediately by a menacing growl and sickening powerful CRUNCH. Experience had taught Holden that the silence that followed such horrific sounds was a sure sign he needed to get the hell out of there.

Holden ran. He passed the Buick with the blinking tail light, skidded around the now smoldering buildings, and bolted for his dog sled.

The dogs were going nuts. They weren't barking; they were whining. The majority pulled sharply against the snow hook, but some were trying to bite right through the tethers.

Holden was only a few feet from the dog sled when he saw his dropped anchor wiggling loose from the ice. The dogs pulled in unison, and with the next pull they would be free. Not only were the phone and gun in the sled, but he'd be stranded here with whatever had killed the girl and destroyed the town.

Holden increased what little speed he could and dove for the sled. Desperate, he flung himself forward and slid the remainder of the distance across the ice and managed to grab the anchor's rope. At that exact moment, the dogs pulled the anchor free and bolted for the trail. The rope burned quickly through his hands, and he cried out as the anchor split open his palm.

Gripping his bloody hand, Holden managed to stumble to his feet. He could only watch as his dog team, along with his gun and phone, vanished quickly down the trail.

WHUMP.

Something the size of a small car landed in the snow behind him. Holden had never been the type to freeze in combat, but he wasn't entirely sure he wanted to see what had snatched the poor young girl at the hardware store.

He heard a loud crunch of snow underfoot as whatever it was took a step behind him. Instinctively he knew that if he ran, he wouldn't get more than a few feet.

Summoning his courage, he spun around swiftly.

Holden didn't see the animal in its entirety. He only glimpsed the clawed hand that struck him so hard that his upper torso snapped around to face the woods behind him, splitting his spinal cord in half in an instant.

Tom Holden's broken body crumpled to the snow. He felt the cold of ice under his ruined face, and tasted the acrid blood in his mouth.

His last thoughts were of his daughter and how soon he would be seeing her again.

Chapter 1

The Arctic Imperative

—ARCTIC IMPERATIVE CONFERENCE
—Northern Lights Ski Resort
—Girdwood, Alaska

"Hello everyone, I'm Dr. Kate Foster."

She had spoken so loudly into the microphone that the feedback was as deafening as it was painful.

Just perfect.

Kate lifted her chin ever so slightly, lowered her volume and flashed her best smile.

You can do this.

"The Arctic Ice Cap covers an area twice as big as the United States, but has been melting at an average rate of twelve percent per decade since 1979. One result of this process is that beneath this dwindling ocean of pack ice, we are discovering landmass and artifacts of long lost civilizations that have not seen the light of day for over ten thousand years."

A few people in the audience perked up at this.

See, there you go.

She wasn't vain but archaeologist Kateland Foster had learned long ago how to dress to impress. When your existence depended on grants, it was a matter of necessity. She had used the last of her grant money to cut her long nutmeg locks down to shoulder length and outfit herself in business attire worthy of the presidents, ambassadors, admirals, and other dignitaries sitting in the room before her. Since she was a little girl, Kate had been often told she was pretty, but at this conference she felt like a short, plump toad compared to the beautiful aides and waitresses, looking more like supermodels, amongst the attendees.

At least I got their attention.

Kate had finally gotten her turn at the podium after two days of listening to countries fight over who owned what in the melting sea of ice of the great Arctic.

Having caught their attention but knowing she could lose it again, she hastily glanced at her note cards and continued. "Unlike in the Yucatan, where orbiting satellites can detect potential dig sites beneath the ground vegetation, satellites are unable to detect manmade rock formations beneath the ice's featureless landscape." She took another controlling breath before continuing. "I think we can all agree that new shipping lanes, Arctic sea ports, drilling platforms, and tourist destinations are all very important. And to think that the Northwest Passage that the British have been searching for over the past six hundred years will be finally realized in our lifetimes." Kate swiped a hand across her forehead and whisked away imaginary sweat. "Whew." Several audience members chuckled at this and she found the majority now smiling back. She was winning them over. Kate smiled warmly and said in her most charming voice, "I've even learned that sailing over the North Pole will be twice as fast as sailing down and back from the Panama Canal. And let's not forget how the Arctic helps defend America." *Give a quick salute to Brigadier General Barton.* When she did, the general's chest swelled slightly.

Kate switched to her more serious tone. "But what about the indigenous inhabitants of the Arctic? Will their cultures be lost forever? I think not. My colleagues have already shared with you the stresses on the Arctic's native peoples, but I'm here to build on the ancestry of not only indigenous peoples but possibly for all of humanity."

Kate glanced at the timer on the podium. Each speaker was only allowed ten minutes before an annoying little red light started flashing silently to let the speaker know to wrap it up in thirty seconds or less. *Damn, two minutes on the stupid introduction; better get right to the good stuff.* She reached for the remote and clicked her first photo. Appearing up on the big screen overhead was a picture of a tiny Russian flag attached to a sunken buoy resting on the murky sea floor. "Here is a photo of a Russian sub planting their flag on the Arctic Ocean floor in 2007, thus marking the beginning of exploration of the Arctic seabed."

At this the Russian ambassador stopped ogling the waitress, put down his Coke, heavy with rum, and smiled wolfishly up at her.

Like most experienced speakers, Kate had developed a system of knowing just how interested guests were in her lectures. For her, it was how many times audience members reached for their water glasses or checked an incoming text.

She was losing them.

Kate clicked again.

Time to bring in the big guns.

"Here we see photographs taken last year by a team of Chinese geologists in their submersible at a depth of 1,500 feet. They were studying tectonic plates on the Alaskan ice shelf approximately twenty-six miles off the north shore of Prudhoe Bay, Alaska."

Faster Kate, faster...

Kate quickly clicked through several photos of underwater seafloor. "Then, after becoming slightly disoriented due to a small onboard navigation malfunction, they stumbled across this solid jade marker underwater."

The next photo was an image of a heavily worn stone totem pole also sitting on the seafloor. With a little imagination, one could even make out figures etched into the stone column.

The clinking glasses fell dead silent and everyone went still. Even the supermodel waitresses.

Gotcha.

Kate thumbed up another slide of the jade totem, this time a wider shot of the underwater totem on a rocky shelf overlooking an abyss.

"We estimate that this landmass was once above ground just before the last Ice Age." *Easy, Kate, control your breathing, don't lose them now. You don't want to come across as some kind of conspiracy theorist nut job.* "And as many of you know, stone totems are very rare amongst Arctic natives and only the earliest of some Alaskan natives ever constructed them at all. But a totem pole made of jade is unprecedented."

The audience leaned forward in their seats and oohed and aahed as she clicked several more photos of the undersea jade totem.

Kate turned towards the audience once. "But that's not all." She brought up more photographs of massive stone walls underwater.

"These geologists appear to have stumbled across the remnants of what seems to be a city the size of Manhattan with massive walls and plazas scattered across a large area of seabed."

Kate paused, scanning the room. "The geologists brought back a sample, and carbon dating indicates that some of the manmade structures are as old as ten thousand years. That's five thousand years older than any ancient city in the world! Was this a lost flooded civilization that flourished before the last Ice Age? Perhaps we may very well find the cradle of civilization hidden within this ancient domain."

Time to bring it home.

"Clearly this is the work of some earlier civilization, and bears further study."

When Admiral Mace raised his hand in question, Kate acknowledged him with a nod.

"So where did this city come from?"

Kate nodded and smiled. "Great question, Admiral. You see, the ancient coastal cities flourished before the last Ice Age. But when the ice caps melted, the sea levels rose four hundred feet, obliterating coastal cities. All traces vanished beneath the sea."

Her enthusiasm became infectious, and a smartly-dressed elderly woman raised her hand. "How old did you say you estimate this underwater city to be?"

"Carbon dating on artifacts recovered from the citadel date back to 7500 BCE That's over 9,500 years old! These discoveries could literally rewrite history."

Sweet silence. She could not have hoped for better.

The host standing at a podium off to the side abruptly interjected, "The chair recognizes the honorable Ragnar Grondal."

Kate glanced over at the president of Iceland. Even seated, he was clearly taller than the average man, and his suit alone probably would've funded her research another full year. She noted that President Grondal wore a look of disdain on his face.

Uh-oh. I have a bad feeling ...

He spoke with only a slight Icelandic accent. "I'm sorry, Doctor ..." Grondal glanced at his notes as if to demonstrate he'd already forgotten her name, dismissed it as unimportant. "Foster, but I'm well aware of this Chinese expedition you speak of and its purely theoretical findings. And I haven't seen anything that makes me believe we've discovered any sort of ancient civilization."

Uh-oh, time to redirect.

Kate opened her mouth to offer a rebuttal, but President Grondal continued in his polite but overpowering way. "In fact, my expert panel of marine archaeologists have dismissed your underwater city as nothing more than natural rock formations, not anything built by man. Some have even compared your jade totem to the photograph of the face on Mars, a trick of shadows, nothing more." Grondal chuckled, and when he glanced around the room, several snickered along with him. "I mean, do you have any further proof? Or is it only sensationalized photo angles that might be used to promote book sales or fund your research?"

Kate felt her cheeks flush. *Geez, what a class A jerk.* She took a deep breath and attempted to gather her thoughts. "The Chinese expedition did report finding similar structures, but their underwater cameras were damaged during the expedition, and they had to return to port. When they returned to the site, they found the totem vanished, presumably during one of the underwater quakes that frequent the area."

At this, Grondal raised his bushy white eyebrows. "Ah, I see ... so after surviving twelve thousand years, *now* the earthquakes decide to destroy your, uh, how do I put this… Atlantis of the North." More laughs from the audience. "And I take it these fantastical photos are the only proof that this jade totem ever existed in the first place?" Grondal tossed his glasses on the table before him, leaned back in his chair, and massaged his weary eyes, as if exhausted by the whole affair.

The red light began flashing on the podium. She attempted to redirect with photos from other dig sites, but the remote control suddenly became very uncooperative. By the time she was able to bring up the next photo of ruins being excavated from a glacier, the podium light had gone steady red, indicating that she was out of time. The impressive photo came into view just as the house lights brightened, obliterating it from view.

In a booming voice, the host said "Thank you, um, Dr. Foster."

No one clapped.

The noise she made gathering up her notes seemed deafening.

The host turned to the crowd. "If everyone would adjourn to the dining room for lunch, we will continue to hear from Rear Admiral Dean Mace on upgrading the Coast Guard to improve Arctic response readiness."

As everyone filed out, Kate, more disappointed than furious, quietly collected her notes and stepped down off the podium.

Damn.

—— < > ——

Kate didn't see the white-haired, bespectacled woman, elegantly dressed, sitting at the back of the room, studying her intently.

"I like this girl," she said to herself in a slight Danish accent. "I think she would be the perfect addition to our research facility on Dead Bear Island." She turned her attention to the small, smartly attired female aide sitting beside her. "Introduce yourself to young Kate. Inform her that an anonymous benefactor would like to fund her research for the next two years and quadruple her grant, effective immediately."

"Offshore or Swiss?" the aide asked immediately, typing notes into the personal computer on her wrist.

"Oh, I don't know. Surprise me," she responded.

"Right away, Ma'am," the aide replied, and then glided efficiently away to carry out her mistress's bidding.

Kate's new benefactor sat alone, reflecting. *If only this Doctor Foster really knew what had happened to her underwater city and caused the Chinese sub to perform an emergency surface. What historians didn't know could fill the Library of Alexandria. What the world didn't know will one day kill every last man, woman, and child on the planet.*

Chapter 2

Welcome to Deadhorse!

The flying building adorned with propellers and wings was named *The Endeavor*. And much like her infamous predecessor that had carried Shackleton through the frozen seas of the South Pole in 1914, the rugged plane knifed her way through the mysterious region of the Great White North.

Where Shackleton's fir-timbered ship had to navigate the dense clusters of giant icebergs; this modern counterpart flew through seventy-five-mile hurricane-force winds guarding the northernmost tip of Alaska.

However, unlike Shackleton's doomed crew who had to endure blistering cold, snow blindness, dysentery, and starvation, the three-engine DC-10 (the third engine being at the base of the tail) carried its passengers in relative comfort, suffering only from cramped seating, stale recycled air, impatient flight attendants, and limited rations of snacks.

When the cabin lurched suddenly, one dozing passenger banged her head on the window where she was napping.

Owwww!

Kate Foster awoke with a start and rubbed the fresh bump on her head. She had passed out asleep immediately after takeoff and was still groggy from the effects of the Dramamine she had taken prior to departure. She had to take a moment to remember where she was.

The binder left open on her tray table was a good clue. It detailed the Arctic research facility that was her final destination. The facility, formerly a deep sea underwater laboratory, had been transported by Chinook helicopter to a tiny island in the Arctic Ocean some twenty-six miles off the northernmost tip of Alaska. According to her brief, the dig site had been chosen due to several undisclosed finds on the island and surrounding seafloor. She was being hired to assist with the excavation and cataloging of all relics.

After her dismal performance at the Arctic Imperative conference, Kate was surprised she still had a job at all. The press had taken Grondal's derogatory description of her work as "The Atlantis of the North" and run with it, even citing her as the lost city's discoverer. The front page of the *Anchorage Daily News* even went so far as to print a very unflattering photo of her at the podium with a surprised look on her face. She hadn't even remembered making that face. Anyway, as far as she was concerned, she was now the laughing stock of the archaeological community.

If there was one silver lining in this latest dismal chapter of her life, she at least had a job, and one in the field at that. She still hadn't figured out who her latest benefactor was, but how does that old saying go? *Don't look a gift horse in the mouth?* Previously, all her studies had been conducted strictly in the warmth and safety of university labs and offices. She had never actually been north of the Arctic Circle before, but she knew she'd be fine. An intern from the research team was supposed to greet her at the terminal and would personally escort her to the research facility. *No problem.* It was at this moment of bolstering her confidence that Kate noticed the price tag still on her Arctic jacket. Glancing around to see if anyone else had noticed the label branding her a tourist, she quickly snapped it off and stuffed it inside her pocket.

DING.

"Folks, this is your captain speaking. As you can tell, we're experiencing some pretty heavy turbulence, not uncommon for this time of year, but the good news is it's not a crosswind and happens to be blowing right down the runway into Deadhorse. So, for the remainder of the trip we're going to have to ask you to raise your seats and tray tables and we will be discontinuing all courtesy service for the duration of the trip." There was another jolt of turbulence, and the pilot's voice came back on a second later, this time in a more serious, less encouraging tone. "Flight crew, please take your seats."

When Kate had first boarded, she had noted that the majority of the passengers bound for the North Slope were rugged oil field workers: scraggly beards, calloused hands, tattoos, all dressed in durable working-man clothes. But she found their demeanor surprisingly professional. Kate attributed this to the fact that even the lowest paid North Slope worker averaged around a minimum of thirty-five bucks an hour and she was certain none of them wanted to do anything to jeopardize their excellent wages.

Another drop in altitude sent her binder crashing to the floor, a harsh reminder to put away her notes and raise her tray table as instructed. As she reached for the dropped binder, she noticed her seatmate's white-knuckled hand clenched in a death grip on the armrest between them.

The man sitting beside her was tall, clean-shaven, good-looking, and about forty. His dark hair was cut short, and his face suggested a roadmap of untold adventures despite the chiseled features. He wore a shirt and tie under a black sports Jameset, but the professional attire did little to mask his athletic frame. *A domesticated lion,* was Kate's first thought. He was also sweating profusely and wore an expression of terror. Clearly, this man did not enjoy flying.

She felt badly for him, and while she was being truthful with herself, maybe she wanted to flirt with him a little too. So, she leaned over to him and whispered, "You know they say that flying is still the safest form of…"

"Save it, lady," he said curtly, without even so much as a sideward glance.

Why is it all the good-looking ones are always rude or married? Spotting the gold band on his ring finger, she added, *and this one's both. And Mom wonders why I'm still single.* The memory of her fiancé cheating on her caused nausea that no amount of Dramamine could cure.

Sitting across the aisle from the good-looking rude guy was another couple, or at least another man and woman. If they were a couple, the man was way over-chicked. He had long greasy bangs that hung over his eyes, a pointed nose, and a pasty-white complexion. He had a gizzard neck, and wore mismatched clothes that hung loosely on his scrawny body. The woman sitting beside him was a smartly-dressed blonde with spikey hair over a pretty but determined face.

Kate noted the spikey-blonde was reading a magazine while the scrawny guy was hunched over his laptop ... on his tray table.

Didn't he hear the captain's announcement?

Kate glimpsed the images scrolling away on scrawny guy's computer. They were gruesome. One photo was of a bloody disemboweled corpse that didn't have a head or limbs. Another snapshot appeared to be human remains smeared all over the wall like a painting by some sort of macabre artist.

As though sensing her gaze, the spikey-blonde glanced up tersely from her magazine and saw Kate peeping at her companion's laptop. She flashed Kate a narrowed glance then nudged the scrawny guy with her elbow.

Scrawny guy was so absorbed in his photos that he nearly jumped out of his seat when she nudged him. Catching Spike's drift, he quickly slammed the lid to his computer closed, and folded his arms defensively over his chest. Spike shook her head in disapproval then returned to her magazine, the latest issue of *Rifle Shooter*.

What kind of sick people am I flying with? Cultists, Satanists? Kate wasn't sure what she found more disturbing: the creepy scrawny guy viewing snuff photos, or that the spikey-haired woman was so nonchalant about it.

A plane full of roughnecks, a good-looking rude guy, and the weirdo couple. This is a regular flying circus. She made a mental note to steer clear of the freak show when they landed, if they landed, and to find her ride out to the island research facility as quickly as possible.

Chapter 3

Airport Terminal

The initial descent had been anything but smooth, but good as his word, the Captain had ridden the hurricane-force winds right down to the runway and set the aircraft mercifully down at Deadhorse Airport without so much as a scratch.

Outside the window, Kate saw a world of gray. The ice fog made visibility less than a dozen feet and she felt lost in it. She could barely make out the airport terminal that appeared out of the mist like a ghost ship.

Kate disembarked the plane, stepped down the mobile stairwell on shaky legs, and stood upon the open tarmac. The blistering winds blowing across icy landscapes was a chilly slap in the face of reality ... she had arrived at the Arctic Circle. With her first breath, the cold seemed to reach inside her lungs and carve her heart out of her chest. She was reminded that the Arctic was a nearly impossible place to survive. She found it difficult to understand how a landscape that was so vast could be so claustrophobic, and felt as though the cold was not only crushing her body from all sides, but also her very soul.

Without further delay, Kate quickly followed the other passengers into the airport terminal. She knew the town of Deadhorse was located at the northernmost edge of Alaska, that there were only about fifty year-round residents, but that number had grown to nearly four thousand when the oil workers who serviced the oilfields of Prudhoe Bay arrived.

To Kate, Deadhorse Airport terminal was little more than a large warehouse. Although attempts had been made to make the interior a tad cheerier, with plenty of faux green shrubbery and vibrant colors on the walls, Kate found the terminal metallic, dusty, and impersonal.

Inside, big oil workers stampeded around her, eager to get to their high-paying jobs. Unsure of her own direction, Kate was just standing there when one oversized roughneck bumped into her without so much as an "Excuse me." She spun around from the impact and dropped her luggage.

As she struggled to recover her bags amongst the running of the bulls, Kate saw a tall, lanky armed security guard standing off to one side. He was wearing a ballcap labeled SECURITY over bottle-cap glasses and had a thin blondish mustache.

She shoved her way over to the security guard and asked, "Excuse me, uh," squinting to see his name tag pinned to his shirt about a foot higher than she was tall, "Sgt. Jenkins. Could you please tell me where ..." She fumbled for the piece of paper with the research assistant's name written on it. The guard watched her bemusedly as she frantically searched her oversized coat pockets. The coat price tag spilled out of her pocket first, but eventually Kate found the note. Sighing, she read, "Sanjay Patel?"

"Well, Ma'am," the security guard began in a thick Alabama accent, "Do you know which camp Mr. Patel is staying at?" He blinked twice behind his bottle-cap glasses waiting for her answer.

"Camp?" Kate asked, confused, then realized. "Oh, he's not staying at any of the oil camps. He's a researcher."

The happy bemused grin on the guard's face dropped and his mood became dour, but despite his betraying face he added cheerfully, "I'm sorry, Ma'am, I don't know anyone by that name, but if you give me a minute, I'll be happy to escort you over to billeting, and we'll see if we can't find out where your friend is located." Then, seeing someone in the crowd he recognized, he said, "Pardon me, Ma'am," and stepped around her. In a much louder voice, the security guard yelled over the crowd, "Detective Decker, James Decker. Over here," he said, waving jubilantly.

Kate turned and saw the good-looking rude guy from the plane walking towards them. He had donned a heavy Arctic coat and easily carried a worn, heavy-duty gear bag slung over one shoulder that only confirmed her domestic lion theory. Through his open coat, she saw a holstered gun and gold badge on his belt along with a few other black leather pouches she didn't recognize. Unlike the roughneck herd whose heads were all pointed forward with stout determination, the detective's head was on a constant swivel. He discreetly took in his surroundings in great detail. When the detective saw the tall lanky Sgt. Jenkins waving at him, he flashed back a look of cheerful recognition.

"Leroy Jenkins," he said. "I didn't know you were up here. What the hell are you doing on the top of the world?"

Sgt. Jenkins grinned from ear to ear. "I got me a nice cushy security job protecting these oil workers from them mean ol' polar bears and wayward tourists." The two men shook hands, and Jenkins added, "Got half the force working up here."

Just then the creepy scrawny guy and spikey-blonde from the plane walked up beside the detective and dropped their own heavy plastic cases.

Man, I just can't get a break.

"Leroy, allow me to introduce you to my criminology team."

Ohhhhh, that explains the gory photos; must be from a crime scene. Kate hadn't realized that the laptop viewing of such gruesome photos had bothered her so greatly until she felt herself relax now.

Spikey-hair stepped forward with her hand firmly outstretched, and Decker said, "This is Detective Bristol Vickers. Vick is an expert in interviews. When she's not slumming around the state solving homicides and missing person cases with me, she teaches behavioral signals and interviewing techniques at the Academy."

"Nice to meet you," Vickers stated professionally.

Decker turned towards Vickers and explained, "Sgt. Jenkins was an instructor at my Trooper Academy down in Sitka. A real hardass, too."

"Ah, Ma'am, don't let him fool you. Ol' Decker here was the poster child for the Troopers, probably the best recruit we ever had."

The creepy guy with oily black bangs down over his face stooped forward and coughed into his hand then offered it to the Sergeant.

Sgt. Jenkins only grimaced slightly as he shook it, and Decker introduced him with slightly less enthusiasm. "And this is Dr. Ian Grimm."

Surprisingly, Sgt. Jenkins piqued up at this. "*The* Doctor Ian Grimm?" he asked with enthusiasm. "As in 'Dr. Death'?"

Kate noted that Dr. Grimm didn't seem to appreciate the reference. He sighed heavily and adjusted his black square-rimmed glasses up onto the bridge of his nose. "Well, yes, I seem to have acquired that nickname."

Jenkins, clearly a fan, nodded his head a couple times, then turned back to the lead detective. "Well, Dex, I'm sure glad you and your team are on this. We ain't never had a murder on the North Slope before, let alone a multiple homicide."

Detective Decker's tone turned serious. "Who is working the North Slope Borough these days?"

Sgt. Jenkins frowned with disapproval before answering, "Tommy Blackwood."

Decker didn't seem to know him. "Is he at the crime scene now?"

Jenkins shook his head. "Hell, no. He's drunk off his ass in his office."

Decker frowned. "You're kidding."

"Wish I was. Ol' Tommy took one look inside, barfed his guts out, and has been hiding out in his office ever since."

Kate was just about ready to give up on Sgt. Jenkins escorting her to billeting when she heard Decker ask, "How far away is the crime scene?"

Before answering, Sgt. Jenkins quickly removed his cap, scratched his yellow peach fuzz haircut and replaced his hat in a manner that suggested it was a nervous habit. "Let's see, Dead Bear Island is about six miles offshore of the West Dock."

Wait a minute, what did he say?

"Excuse me, Sergeant, I couldn't help but overhearing," Kate started to say, but then noticed spike-haired girl ... Detective Vickers, staring at her with narrowed eyes again. Summoning her courage and continuing anyway, she asked, "Did you say there's a multiple homicide on Dead Bear Island?"

Detective Decker frowned, and picking up on his visual cue, Associate Detective Vickers stepped in front of her and asked, "And you would be?"

Kate thrust her hand straight out in front of her, "Oh, sorry. I'm Dr. Kateland Foster. My research facility is on Dead Bear." Then to Sergeant Jenkins she added, "That's where I'm supposed to be going anyway."

The way Detective Decker and the others were all looking at each other and then down at their feet it was almost as if... *Oh God, no. Were those gruesome photos of my team?*

The lead detective moved forward. "I'm sorry, Miss...?"

"Kate," she stammered. And without knowing why she added, "Dr. Kate Foster, actually."

In a much gentler tone than she thought the tall detective capable of, he said, "Dr. Foster, I'm Detective James Decker with the Alaska Bureau of Investigations." They shook hands. He read her face for a reaction then asked, "Did you know the members of the research team?"

Past tense? I think I'm going to be sick.

"Uhmmm, yes. I've worked with Sierra and Eugene Banks before, oh and Bill Peterson, but that was only at the university in Anchorage."

Decker nodded then, and with great reluctance he finally told her. "I'm sorry, Dr. Foster, but your friends were killed some time during the last twenty-four hours." He waited for her reaction. When she offered none, too stunned to react, he continued, "We're still hazy on the details, but that's why we're here. We're going to go out to the facility on the island and find out what happened."

"Let me go with you," she blurted out. *What am I doing? Didn't you hear him when he said all of your friends were murdered?*

Decker immediately responded. "I'm sorry, but that isn't remotely possible. The facility is a closed crime scene. I would suggest you get back on the plane and take the next flight back down to Anchorage."

No one was more shocked than Kate herself when she refused to give up without a fight. "Listen, I've got valuable research out there. And if everyone's dead, you're going to need a representative of the property, won't you?" The detective didn't seem convinced.

Vickers, an unlikely ally, leaned closer to him and said under her breath, "Look Dex, she might be able to help ID some of the bodies."

Kate took a step closer to Decker, and without meaning to, rested a hand on his forearm. "Look, Detective Decker, I can't let my team have died out there for nothing."

Decker thought about it for a moment longer, rubbed his jaw, then stabbed a finger towards her. "Okay, but you do exactly what I say, when I say it. You stand exactly where I tell you to stand and you don't touch anything."

"No problem. You won't even know I'm there."

Sgt. Jenkins then interjected, "I can either show you to your rooms, or, if you're hungry, I can take you to the cantina for some chow."

Dr. Grimm, quiet since his introduction, spoke up from behind. "If it's all the same to you, Sergeant, I'd like to get out to the crime scene straight away."

Kate found herself wondering if Grimm was being professional or just morbidly excited to get to the gore.

Sgt. Jensen replied, "Sorry, Dr. Grimm, but we just upgraded to Phase II, White Out conditions. No one moves anywhere unless traveling in a convoy."

Decker turned towards the Sergeant. "Well then, Leroy, what are you waiting for? Let's form up a convoy and get the hell out there."

Sgt. Jenkins removed his cap, scratched his peach fuzz, and replaced it once more before bobbing his head in agreement. "Okay, follow me. We need to get you folks in some heavier survival gear. Then we'll head over to the vehicle pool."

As the Sergeant led them back outside of the terminal and into the frigid elements Kate gripped her Jameset tighter before stepping out to follow them.

What happened out there? And what did they find that was worth killing them over?

Chapter 4

Vehicle Pool

Kate had once read that above the Arctic Circle, the indigenous people had twenty-four hours of darkness during the winter. This was not true, at least not completely. During the winter months, the sun never quite breaches the horizon, but it does get almost twilight outside during the day.

And there isn't as much snow as one might think, either. Many days, the temperature is far too cold to snow, or the heavy winds blow most of the snow away, leaving only ice. That was the case now. It was twenty below, which Vickers explained to Kate was moderate for the time of year.

Before heading out to the research facility, Detective Decker had wanted to stop by the North Slope Borough Police Department in Deadhorse. The office was only a few minutes down the road from the airport terminal and well marked by reflective markers.

On the ride over in heavy-duty pickup patrol vehicles, Vickers explained to Kate that the North Slope Borough officially had jurisdiction, but it was customary to check in with the local authorities before pursuing an active investigation. "Think of him as the Sheriff of this one-horse town."

To Kate, the North Slope Borough Police station resembled every other building in the Arctic: storage containers with windows. However, no two were *exactly* alike: some were fat, others long, all different colors and all a variety of heights. It was like some giant toddler had dropped his colored blocks in the snow.

When they had entered the Borough cop's office, Decker and his team had found Officer Tommy Blackwood sobbing away at his desk with an empty bottle of whiskey clasped in his hand.

Kate found herself slipping in and out of reality, wondering if this was all just some crazy dream. Thus far, her entire visit to the Arctic seemed so surreal to her. What she did remember was that when Detective Decker questioned him, the Borough cop only managed, "I just handle fish and game violations and illegal drinking, maybe even a DV now and then, but I'm not trained to handle anything like this."

When Decker had told Tommy he would lose his job for drinking on duty, especially since alcohol is strictly forbidden on the North Slope, Tommy replied, "I don't give a crap. They can fire my ass, but I sure as hell ain't going back out there."

At least it's not like in the movies, Kate mused, *where the cops are always fighting over jurisdiction.*

After the brief visit with Tommy the Slope cop, Sgt. Jenkins drove them over to the vehicle pool, basically an oversized garage with lots of big boy toys in it. Sgt. Jenkins stood between two giant-sized Arctic Sno-Cat tractors. Each rig sported big fiberglass cabs balanced on shock absorbers which were then mounted on two sets of oversized rubber tank treads. Jenkins explained that they wouldn't need a boat to get out to Dead Bear Island because the ice pack was so thick this time of year that they could just drive over the frozen water in the tractors.

Before boarding, however, the Sergeant outfitted each of them with the proper Arctic gear. Snow bunny-boots with rubber soles, thick parkas, neoprene face masks, and safety googles over layers and layers of clothes, so much so that when Kate walked out of the locker room, she felt like the Michelin Man in those tire commercials.

Sgt. Jenkins had also organized a quick safety briefing in the hanger. He showed Decker the latest satellite images of fissures under the snow between the mainland and the island. Hunkered over an oversized map on a workbench, he explained, "We can avoid the cracks in the ice by setting up way points on our GPS systems. I've already plotted a course around the existing fissures."

Decker grinned at the man. "Nice work, Sergeant. You do good work."

Jenkins removed his cap then replaced it. "Naw, I'm just a dumb yokel from down south. I was just due for an atta-boy, is all."

Kate didn't buy the Sergeant's act anymore. For whatever reason, the Sergeant tried to pass himself off as an idiot, but clearly that summary of the sergeant's skills couldn't have been further from the truth.

"I'd love to take you guys over in the hovercraft, but anything over twenty-five knots and she's about as stable as a kite in a hurricane."

"How long will it take us to get out to the island in the tractors?" Kate asked.

"Well, Ma'am, the island's just under thirty-two miles off the mainland. Best possible safe speed on the ice is around eight miles an hour."

Quickly doing the math Decker answered, "Four hours at best, eh?"

"Yeah, and that's if one of us doesn't get stuck, and has to be winched out by the other one."

Grimm stepped forward and asked, "What if we both get stuck?"

Sgt. Jenkins blinked twice behind his bottle-cap glasses and answered, "In Phase II conditions like this? Depending on how long the storm lasts, we'd be in really big trouble."

"Geez, Sergeant. You're a regular ray of sunshine," Kate said.

Grimm flashed a dour expression, which pretty much summed up how Kate felt about the Sergeant and his constant need to freak them out.

"What about the weather? We gonna catch a break?" Decker inquired.

"There's a second storm front on the way but we should reach the facility long before it gets here. Right now, the wind has decreased to thirty miles an hour, and visibility is little more than twenty feet, but there's no sign of the storm abating." The Sergeant removed his cap and replaced it. "It's basically now or maybe next week."

"Well," Decker said, patting the Sergeant on the back, "We'd best make it now."

And with that, two of Sgt. Jenkins's security men immediately climbed aboard the first tractor.

When Jenkins and Decker threw open the hanger door and let the wind inside, Kate was eager to climb up into her own heated cab to get out of the frigid winds.

Decker climbed nimbly up the treads and was about to jump inside the passenger side door when he noticed Kate struggling in her thick layers of clothes to climb aboard. "Here," he said, offering a hand. When she took it, he hoisted her up off her feet effortlessly.

"Thanks," Kate said, genuinely appreciative of the assistance.

"No problem." He held the rear door open for her, leaned in a bit and asked, "You sure you want to go through with this? I mean, it's going to be pretty gruesome out there."

Kate knew the detective wasn't just talking about the weather. She felt a lump in her throat and could only nod in reply.

Decker was about to climb into the front passenger seat when Jenkins called, "Dex, you better drive, while I navigate." Sgt. Jenkins glanced to where the first tractor had departed and said, "I don't trust these kids. They'll probably lead us right down a crevice or sumthin'."

Grinning broadly at the thought of driving the big rig, Decker didn't have to be told twice and repositioned himself behind the controls.

Meanwhile, Kate was forced to sit on the rear bench seat between Vick and Grimm.

Decker scrutinized the gauges for a few minutes until satisfied, then announced, "Here we go," and started the tread-wheeled vehicle forward. Its tracks rolled off the cement and onto the ice. The tractor's cab bobbed up and down comfortably on its springs until Decker got a feel for the controls, but it wasn't long before they were moving at a steady pace.

The bright lights on the roof illuminated the blowing snow ahead of them. There wasn't a soul moving, and to Kate, Deadhorse looked like the ghost town its name implied. At the edge of town, Kate watched the first tractor bob down and suddenly disappear.

She leaned forward in her seat and was about to ask what had happened to the other tractor when she realized it had only rolled down a steep embankment and out onto the snowfield.

This frozen wasteland was as terrifying as it was beautiful. As they moved deeper into the frozen wasteland, Kate twisted in her seat and glanced at the town behind them. The falling snow and ice fog had already begun to obscure the lighted buildings. And in a moment, even those completely vanished into the mist.

In Kate's mind, they might as well have been sojourning across the surface of the moon.

Chapter 5

Pack Ice

For nearly four hours, the Arctic tractors trundled onward immune to the harsh weather that dumped on them from angry northern skies. With the sergeant navigating, Decker drove expertly around wall formations, jagged crystalline peaks, and cracks on the ice pack.

At first, Kate had been grateful to be inside the warm cabin, but the tractor's contented bobbing, the noise of the little whirring fan on the heater, and the feeling of warmth it produced combined to cause her to doze off. The view outside didn't help much either. In all directions, it was little more than white, white, some gray, and even more white. How Decker could see where he was going in the ice fog, she had no idea. As she drifted in and out of consciousness, she listened to the two men up front talking.

"You already clear the facility?" Decker asked.

Sgt. Jensen nodded. "Yes, sir. First thing. Whoever or whatever killed those people was long gone by the time we got there. We tried our best not to step in anything but, uh, it was kind of hard not to." His hat came off, then back on, he spit dip in an empty water bottle and, said "It's probably best if you just see for yourself."

Squishing Kate as she did so, Detective Vickers leaned forward between the two front seats and asked, "When you first arrived, were there any tracks outside the facility?"

"Nope. Even if there had been, they'd already be gone. This kind of storm, with the wind blowing, you lie down in the snow and they wouldn't find your body till next spring."

There's a cheery thought, Kate thought. She realized suddenly that she had to pee like a racehorse. Her abdomen could feel each bump as they bounced along over another series upon series of ice ridges. "Will it be much longer?" she asked, struggling to keep the hope out of her voice.

"According to the GPS, it ain't much farther," the Sergeant assured. "Gotta be less than a half mile now."

Grimm leaned over to Kate and whispered, "He's been saying that for the last forty minutes."

"Quit griping, Grimm," Vickers mumbled, and resumed staring out the window.

"I'm not," Grimm whined back. "I'm just tired of being cooped up in this bouncing tin can." He traced a sad face in the condensation on his window. "I think it's ludicrous it's taken us nearly half the day just to drive thirty-two miles."

The tractor suddenly tilted back and they started traveling on an upwards slope. Kate could see an enormous wooden dock, barely visible in the mist. She was reminded of the fact that the facility was on an island and that the ice they had been traveling over was normally ocean water during the summer months. Kate stared at the thick-timbered dock enshrined in ice as the tractor trundled by it. Had the manmade structure not been there, she would have had a hard time differentiating the island from the pack ice surrounding it. She wondered if visitors to the island during the dead of winter ever took a wrong turn and simply walked out to open sea.

A few minutes later, Sgt. Jenkins announced in his most southern drawl yet. "Here we are."

Kate leaned forward and followed the direction the Sergeant indicated with the tractor's overhead floodlights. As they approached, details emerged from the ice mist. The spotlight caught the plexiglas built-in windows of a large metallic cylinder in its ethereal landscape.

Decker brought the big tractor to an abrupt stop when they passed the large wooden sign fallen from one of the two four-by-four wooden posts. It read, *Welcome to the Spam Can.*

The lead tractor had already parked and Kate saw the two heavily clad security guards disembarking.

"Welcome to the Spam Can," Sgt. Jenkins announced. The three-storey building resembled just that. Under his breath he muttered, "Where the hell is my guard?" Turning back towards Decker he said, "Hang back here a minute."

Jenkins cracked the door to the tractor and the fierce cold jumped inside. The moment he did, Kate thought her nose was going to flash freeze right off her face.

Kate watched through her window as a copper-faced kid in a dark blue parka jumped out of a third idling tractor already parked out front, and ran over to them.

"Why the hell weren't you at your post?" the Sergeant roared in a manner that surprised Kate.

"I was cold as hell, sir," the kid answered. "Main power went out a couple hours ago. Now it's just auxiliary power keeping it barely warm enough to keep the pipes from freezing."

Unlike everyone else Kate had seen working on the slope, this kid appeared to be only in his early twenties. She also noted he was carrying a shotgun slung across his chest.

Comforting, as long as he doesn't shoot any of us by accident.

"I don't give a damn," the Sergeant yelled back. "That's why you're wearing Arctic gear. No one had better gone inside."

"Yes sir," the kid stammered, then said, "No, sir. No one's been in or out except me." His face then turned somber. "Look, Sarge, I've been hearing some creepy things out here."

"Creepy things, like what?"

"I dunno, like moaning or something."

"Moaning, or something," the Sergeant mocked, "That's just the wind, kid."

"No, Sarge, it ain't the wind. I know what the wind sounds like. When I was a kid, my grandfather used to take me hunting on the ice. We would go way beyond the village all the time. And I'm telling ya, the ice, the way it's creaking back and forth, it ain't, I dunno, it ain't natural."

The Sergeant yelled something else, but the wind took it away and Kate only caught part of it, which involved obscenities. The native youth quickly straightened up and resumed his post by the main entrance.

When the Sergeant returned, he hiked a thumb towards the young guard, and explained with a disapproving scowl, "That's Nikko. He's the captain's kid."

Before Kate exited the safety and warmth of the tractor, Sgt. Jenkins barred her path. "Ma'am, you might want to wait here. It's mighty horrific inside."

Did she really want to go in there? She personally knew three of the victims. How was she going to react when she saw their dead bodies? Would she throw up? Pass out? Summoning her best tough-gal voice she replied, "I didn't ride out all this way to sit in the cab, Sergeant."

Huh, that almost sounded convincing even to me.

When she saw Decker exiting without switching off the engine, she asked, "Wait a minute? Aren't you going to kill the engine? What if we run out of gas?"

Decker glanced over at her. "Shut the engine in these temperatures and the engine might not start again. Ever."

Stiff from the journey, everyone slowly clambered down from the tractor tires and into the snow. The short trek was difficult because the snow blowing in from the prevailing winds had piled up into snow drifts on all sides.

Closing in on the main entrance, Kate could see the bear cage built around the exit. The enclosure around the main entrance reminded her of the shark cages she had seen on television. She knew the bear cage was designed so that a person could exit the building, safely check their surroundings, and not get ambushed by a bear.

"So much for the bear cage," Vickers proclaimed.

Kate had been watching her footsteps so she didn't immediately catch what Vickers was talking about.

"What could have done this?" Decker asked. "These things are rated for a thousand-pound polar bear."

"I know, right?" Jenkins asked, then spit some more dip in his water bottle.

Walking up between the two men, Kate finally saw it. Someone, or something, had pried back the metal bars of the bear cage. Additionally, a heavy steel hatch was hanging off the doorframe, allowing snow to blow inside the structure's arctic entry.

Kate began to shiver uncontrollably. Even beneath the layers of clothing, she was starting to feel the cold. Dr. Grimm somehow seemed oblivious. He was fascinated by the bent bars and broken door and studied them intently. With great difficulty, he clumsily removed his digital camera from one of his many insulated carrying cases and began filming.

To be heard above the wind, Sgt. Jenkins announced loudly, "We tried to close the outer door to protect the integrity of the crime scene, but the metal's bent back so bad we couldn't move it."

The Sergeant turned and was about to head inside when Decker grabbed him by the elbow and yelled into his ear, "And you're sure whoever did this still isn't inside?"

The Sergeant blinked two times before answering. "Pretty sure."

Decker shook his head. He then threw his hood back, unzipped his parka, and in practiced moves, drew his Glock pistol and flashlight. He stepped cautiously over the doorframe's raised threshold. He paused briefly, listening for the sound of movement, and then ducked under the yellow crime scene tape across the open door and was gone.

Kate knew she had two choices. She could either stay outside, pee in her pants, and then freeze to death, or she could follow Decker inside, use the facilities, and witness the horrors within. Feeling the urging of her bladder and the uncontrollable shivering of her body, she gingerly stepped inside.

Chapter 6

Arctic Entry

It took a moment for Kate's eyes to adjust to the darkness inside the arctic entry. The narrow room was bare, little more than bench seats and heavy coat hangers lining the walls.

Before she could fully comprehend what was inside, she felt a pair of strong hands grab her shoulders from behind.

A harsh whisper in her ear said, "Try not stepping in the blood." It was Detective Decker.

Kate gazed at her feet. When she lifted her foot, she saw her boot print on a frozen puddle of congealed blood on the floor.

Decker shined his flashlight through the interior hatch and scanned inside the facility. He gave her a sidelong glance. "Won't even know you're here, huh?"

"Sorry," she stammered, then her anger pooling she grumped, "It's my first time at a crime scene, okay?"

"Just wait here until the Sergeant and I have a chance to check the building one more time."

Before he and the Sergeant could leave her, Kate asked, "Wait a minute? You're leaving us down here, alone?"

"Don't worry, you're not alone," Decker intoned, "You've got Vick, Nikko, and Grimm right behind you."

The Sergeant leaned his head and added, "Yeah, and you've also got two more of my guys stationed outside."

She heard herself respond with a meek, "Okay," but they had already gone inside.

Through the open hatchway Kate could see the main lights were not on. And there was no way of telling how long auxiliary power had been draining the batteries. Even within the shadows, she could see the unmistakable frozen stains of sticky blood painted across the floor. She could also see overturned tables and chairs, but that was about the extent she could make out from the arctic entry.

She rubbed her shoulders for warmth. With the main power offline and the outer hatch still open, she was still shivering and seeing her own breath.

Vick and Grimm suddenly entered the tight-fitting arctic entry with their heavy equipment cases and crowded past her.

"Oh, geez." It was Grimm.

"What's the matter now?" Vickers asked, annoyed. She didn't even try to hide her contempt for the man.

Grimm was staring at her boot print. "We're not even on scene for sixty seconds and she's already contaminated the crime scene."

"I'm sorry," Kate began, but to her surprise, Vickers jumped to her aide.

"Hey, give her a break. These people were her friends."

That shut up "Doctor Death." At least for a little while anyway. Still, he didn't look too happy about it.

Kate glanced at a map of the facility mounted on the wall. From her brief, she remembered the base was three storeys tall. The first floor was the main laboratory. The second was personnel quarters with a large common area that included a kitchen, rec hall, and dining area. And on the third floor was the comm center, base operations, and an observatory.

About a minute later, Decker stuck his head back inside and spoke to all of them. "All right, you can come in the main room, but try to stay in the center of the room until we have a chance to clear the outer rooms on the first floor."

They all eagerly exited the frigid arctic entry and entered the main facility through the inner hatch. The thick hatch and the steel-riveted walls were a good reminder that the facility had originally been an undersea lab. Kate took only one small step inside, careful not to step in any more blood.

Other than the fierce winds outside and glittering debris of shattered glass crunching beneath her feet, the only sound was her owned labored breath. She was relieved to find that she could tell it was already a bit warmer in here. When the main power had gone out, the emergency lighting must have kicked in, bathing everything in a supernatural crimson color, reminding her of Hell. Even though she couldn't see much, there was enough light to see that the main room had been totally trashed. A large table was overturned, and hard copies of reports were scattered everywhere. Immediately apparent was blood, spattered on everything.

She could see the sergeant and Detective Decker checking the outer, smaller rooms with their flashlights.

As Nikko entered, he offered nervously, "This much blood. It has to have been a polar bear, right, Sarge? I mean what else could have done something like this?"

The Sergeant responded aloud. "How the hell would a polar bear tear through a steel cage like that? Geez, Nikko. Use your head for somethin' other than holding up your hat."

Psh. Well, sir, then what do you propose tore through that cage, Kate wondered, but kept it to herself.

The other two security guards, laden with more equipment cases, entered single file.

"You can put those over there," Dr. Grimm said in a tone that was more of a command than a request. He indicated a table against the far wall that seemed to be the least unscathed in the room.

Kate saw the guard's faces. The burlier of the two guards, wearing a walrus mustache over a perpetual frown, appeared ready to drop the heavy cases right where he stood. Instead, both men checked with their sergeant. The Sarge's nod indicated it would be acceptable, at least this time, to play the role of bellboy.

The area that Grimm selected would serve as their base of operations. Vickers confirmed this when she put her equipment cases over there as well.

Under the direction of Sergeant Jenkins, the two security guards cleared the snow out of the entrance and secured the inner hatch. Vickers and Nikko found some portable heaters in a closet and placed them about the center of the room. They now had a small base camp in the midst of the blood bath.

Within minutes of the heaters' activation, Vickers unzipped her coat and said, "Man, I'm roasting in this parka." She then took off her gloves and jacket too. Righting a chair, she hung both over it.

Everyone but Kate quickly followed suit. It was certainly much warmer than outside, but until the heaters had a little more time to work their magic, she decided to remove only her gloves and keep her coat on.

Decker and the Sergeant stood on the other side of the room. The Sergeant took his cap off, put it back on, and then asked, "Well, boss, what do you want me and my men to do next?"

Decker said, "First order of business is always survival, right?"

The Sergeant needed no further urging. He turned back to his men and bellowed, "Barton, Alonzo, as soon as you guys are done bringing in the rest of the doctor's equipment, find the maintenance shed and get the generators fueled up and running. The auxiliary batteries aren't going to run forever. I want main power back on within the hour, and keep it running." He then saw Nikko standing there. "Nikko, what the hell do you think you're doing?"

"Helping Detective Vickers with her equipment?" he explained meekly. Despite the differences in their ages, Nikko clearly had some sort of infatuation with the Associate Detective.

"Funny, it looked like you were just standing around with your thumb up your ass. Get your lazy butt back outside and keep those tractors running and topped off with fuel. You want to strand us here permanent-like?"

Kate suppressed a smile. She was an academic who had spent most of her adult life around other academics. She was unaccustomed to being around such rough-and-tumble men. Her colleagues had been scientists. These men were the professionals you called in to deal with emergency situations. And until they figured out what had attacked her team, she felt it slightly comforting.

While the guards brought more of the criminologist's equipment inside, Vick moved over to Decker. Handing him a clipboard she said, "I grabbed this off the wall. Manifest says there should be five people on station: three scientists and two support personnel."

"Does that sound right, Dr. Foster?" Decker asked.

Kate was still in a daze. The blood splatter was starting to freak her out. She had heard the detective's words as though she were on the other side of a tunnel but eventually she replied softly, "Yes, Detective. Three scientists, an intern, and one engineer to keep the lights on."

"We've got lots of blood, but where are the bodies?" asked Grimm aloud.

Sgt. Jenkins frowned and lifted his eyes toward the ceiling.

Decker caught his meaning. "All right, everyone wait here until the Sergeant and I reconnoiter upstairs."

"Want us to come?" Vick asked.

Decker thought for a second. "Nah, you and Grimm finish setting up here. I just want to make sure no one slipped inside past Nikko while he was out here guarding the facility by himself."

Not sure exactly what to do with her hands, Kate clutched her elbows as she watched the two men head for the tiny stairwell.

As the guards set down the equipment, Dr. Grimm asked aloud, to no one in particular, "Hello, anybody home?" When no one laughed, he began to sing softly to himself. "Ewwww, that smell. Can't you smell that smell?"

"Hey, knock that off," Vickers disciplined, and then tossed her head over to Kate.

"What?" Grimm saw Kate's pale face, and added, "Oh, right, I forgot. Civilian ...on ...deck." He pushed his greasy bangs out of his face with one hand and began removing his equipment from their cases, not realizing he was still softly humming the same tune.

But Grimm was right. It did smell funny, and not like dead body funny. "Phew ... smells like rotten eggs in here." As soon as she said it, Kate watched all these big, tough, security men flash a look of panic on their faces. The burly one with the mustache and perpetual grimace asked her with a growl, "What did you just say?"

"I said it smells like rotten eggs in here." Kate sniffed again. "Wait a minute. Now it smells more like sulfur."

The mustached guard, the kid Nikko, and the other guard immediately stopped whatever they were doing and their eyes frantically went to the little boxes pinned to their breast pockets.

"I'm negative," the mustached guard announced with relief.

"Me too," Nikko answered.

"I'm in the green also," the other guard, who looked Hispanic, answered. "Must be some spoiled food in the garbage or sumthin'."

Kate's eyes were wide. Something had really shaken those tough security guys to the core. She turned back around and moved over to Vickers. Out of earshot, she asked, "What was that all about?"

Still unpacking and focusing on her equipment, Vick answered, "Do you see those little boxes pinned to their chests? Those are gas detectors. In the Arctic, sulfur dioxide is a common killer. OSHA's exposure limit is just two parts per million. At higher concentrations, you're dead with your next breath."

"Oh," Kate said, and then took little comfort when she realized she wasn't wearing a gas detector. *But if not poisonous gas, what was causing the smell?*

Suddenly a radio crackled, and Kate could hear Decker's voice come over the speaker.

"Vick, got your ears on?"

Vickers had removed three radios and accompanying radio chargers from one of the heavy plastic equipment cases. She attached one radio to her belt, and then slipped the light wireless headset over her head.

"Yeah, Dex, go ahead."

"We've got at least one body up here on the second floor."

A look of confusion appeared on Vickers's face. "Come back, Dex. Did you say at least one? You're not sure?"

"You'll see when you get up here," he radioed back solemnly.

"Copy that, Dex. You want me to come up or finish unpacking?"

Decker radioed back. "Come on up. You and Grimm can finish setting up downstairs later."

Vickers tipped her head over at Grimm who returned a childish grimace. As she grabbed a flashlight, Decker radioed, "Oh, and if she's up to it, bring Kate, too. Maybe she can ID one of the more intact bodies."

When Vickers raised her eyebrows at Kate in a questioning glance, Kate took a deep breath and nodded back.

Kate fell in line behind Vickers. As they headed for the small stairwell, Kate recalled how Vickers had used Decker's name each time she responded. Not sure why, she wondered if Vickers might be sweet on her boss.

"Hey, don't wait for me, or anything," Grimm complained as he jogged after them.

Chapter 7

2nd Floor

"Where's his head?"

Kate heard these words as she entered the second floor. They came from Sgt. Jenkins. He and Detective Decker were gazing at something obscured by an overturned ping pong table.

That was the first thing Kate heard, but it wasn't the first thing she saw. The first thing she saw was the gaping hole in the wall. The fissure was big enough to drive a small car through.

What could have caused that, a rocket launcher?

Outside the jagged opening, the wind screamed and spewed up piles of snow inside the breach. Kate once more felt the embrace of the frigid air coming in and hugged herself for warmth. She was glad she had decided to keep her jacket on.

Vickers and Grimm were now standing over by Decker when he asked, "Grimm, you rolling on this?"

"Uh, absolutely," Grimm responded. Kate thought Grimm's tone a tad disrespectful. She was no psychologist, but she suspected Grimm had a problem with authority. Any authority. The bony criminologist moved forward, but his eyes were always on the digital display of his camera.

As the criminologists stood gathered around the headless body, Decker turned toward her and asked with concern in his voice, "Dr. Foster, are you up for this?"

Kate knew what he was asking. He wanted her to identify the body. She had never seen a dead body before. The few funerals she had attended had always been closed casket. The only bodies she'd ever seen were on TV or in the movies. She managed to nod, but that was all she could manage.

Her boots crunched broken glass as she moved deeper into the room. Rounding the overturned ping pong table, the first thing she noticed was the body. It didn't appear real. In fact, bodies in the movies seemed more real than this.

The human torso was lying on the floor in the shadows, bloated and beyond recognition. Judging by its girth, it had once been a big man. Whoever he was, he wore durable suspenders over rugged clothes. Where his head should have been, there was a halo of blood. Both legs were gone, as though amputated with a machete, and one arm was completely missing while the other had been severed at the elbow. Kate could see white bone sticking out where the elbow should have been. The torso wasn't even fully intact. The stomach had been ripped out, and what little entrails remained had been smashed into the floor. Every time the wind from the hole outside died down, she got a whiff of decaying flesh. The stench was overpowering, and she immediately shielded her nose and mouth inside her coat.

As her knees began to buckle she felt light-headed and was certain she was going to vomit.

Vickers appeared beside her and slipped a steadying arm around her shoulders. "Easy, Kate. Try to breathe through your mouth."

Taking her advice, Kate found that her nausea became manageable, for the moment.

Studying the body through the lens of his camera, Grimm said aloud to no one in particular, "The teeth sheared straight thru the bone. I mean, what can even do that?"

No one volunteered an answer.

After a long pause, Decker asked her gently, "Dr. Foster, do you recognize him?"

How could she possibly know this lump of flesh? There was barely a torso. She was about to scream that exact thought at the detective but then she saw something metallic lying in the frozen goopy mess. It was a golden belt buckle that read TEXAS.

"Oh … it's …," she could hardly form the words. "It's Bill. Bill Peterson." At the realization that this pile of human waste was someone she actually knew, Kate felt the bile rise up in her throat once more. She forced it back down with controlling breaths. "He was an engineer, kinda like a maintenance man. Kept everything running. I only know it's him because back in Anchorage he always wore that ginormous belt buckle, and … and the overalls."

When no one said anything, Grimm leaned over and whispered to Vick, "Hey Vick, what do you think the cause of death was?"

"Shut up, Grimm," Vickers muttered.

The Sergeant suddenly interjected miserably, "If you think that's bad, wait till you see the hallway."

—— <> ——

In the murky passageway, they had to rely on their flashlights because even the emergency lights had been smashed beyond repair. Only one flickering light bulb remained operable, and it swung from ripped out wires sparking with juice.

The blood trail started in the rec area and continued down the hallway as though painted by some gruesome paint brush. Kate's first impression was that the walls appeared crumpled, as if something too large to fit had forced its way through the corridor anyway.

As the beams of their lights played over the misshapen walls, it took Kate a moment to realize the furry picture on the wall she was staring at was a bloody human scalp smashed into the drywall.

The Sergeant flashed his beam on the opposite wall and indicated with a nod.

Kate gasped when she saw a severed arm sticking out of the drywall. Something obviously very large had shaken someone violently apart in the small passageway.

Detective Decker examined the scalp closer with his light. "Must have taken tremendous force to tear off an arm like that and then get it stuck into the wallboard."

"Well, at least we know it's a woman," Vickers offered.

"How do you know that?" Kate asked, incredulous. It was difficult enough to establish that the remains were human, let alone gender.

"The fingers. Slender and painted with nail polish," Decker answered for her.

Vickers checked the manifest. "Three men and two girls. By process of elimination this is either Sierra Banks or Charlotte Hettersfield."

Kate felt the bile rise up into her throat again. "It's not Sierra." When she saw everyone looking at her she explained, "Sierra's Athabascan. She's got darker skin. That arm is white. Plus Sierra is," she paused for a moment, "was tall. That arm looks like it belongs to a shorter person. Must be her assistant, Charlotte, but I've never met her."

Vickers didn't appear to be listening. Instead she was shining her flashlight up on the blood-spattered ceiling. What was sticking out of the ceiling reminded Kate of boys back in elementary school throwing their pencils up into the air and trying to stick them into the tiles. In this case, it wasn't pencils hanging from the ceiling. It was teeth.

Vickers's probing flashlight beam lit up another section of the ceiling.

"Is that a…?" Vickers started to ask.

But Decker cut her off and said, "That'd be my guess."

Kate saw the remains of a human face pressed onto the ceiling; its eyeless sockets seemed to stare down at her. She held her stomach with one hand and leaned on Decker for support with the other. "Excuse me; I think I need to go to the bathroom." She was too afraid to move, as if taking a single step would cause her stomach to explode out her mouth. Just when she thought she had some semblance of self-control, she noticed the pinkish spongy corded material hanging from the smashed-up face. Kate realized it was the woman's brains. She turned away and was violently sick … multiple times.

Sgt. Jenkins, having anticipated this, had borrowed a wastebasket from a nearby bathroom and held it up for her to vomit in.

Grimm, unsympathetic to her sickness, said with a groan, "Is there any part of the crime scene you aren't going to contaminate?"

"Shut up, Grimm," Vickers barked.

Ignoring Vickers, Grimm theorized aloud and in a clinical tone, "So, something tears through the bear cage guarding the entrance outside, rips off the steel hatch, attacks at least one person downstairs, then climbs up the stairwell to the second floor, attacks poor ol' headless Billy-Bob over there, chases the little intern girl down the hallway, shakes her to pieces, and then jumps out the window?"

Decker turned to Kate. He gave her a questioning glance as she wiped the puke from her mouth. *I'm a regular princess,* she thought sarcastically, but nodded that she was fine. Decker then looked back at Grimm. "A good theory, but I can't say I quite agree with your police work there, Grimm."

Grimm flashed him a look of insult, an unspoken, *Really? So then what's your theory?*

They exited the corridor and moved back out into the rec room with the gaping hole.

Decker passed his hand over the hole, examining the outer jagged edges. "First of all, this hole wasn't made from something punching its way out." For emphasis, he pantomimed punching a fist through it. "Whatever passed through this wall was outside, coming in."

Kate recalled that the first floor of the facility was partially submerged in the island for stabilization. Even though they were technically on the second floor, the ground was only a half-storey down.

Vickers must have been thinking the same thing for she moved up to Decker, leaned her head out of the hole, and gazed downward. She squinted her eyes against the stinging pellets of hail lashing against her face. She had to shout to be heard above the wind. "I don't know, Dex, we've got to be at least nine feet up." Then bringing her head back inside the complex she turned to him and asked, "You really think someone could have jumped that high and crashed through the wall?"

"I'm not saying anyone jumped up nine feet in the air and smashed through anything. I'm saying that whatever made this hole ... did it from the outside coming in."

To illustrate his point further Decker pointed to the floor, "Remember, debris fields don't lie. See how much is on the inside?" When Vickers nodded, the lead detective continued. "Nope. Our perpetrator, or something he used, entered from outside and made this opening in the wall." Decker then moved over to where the headless torso lay. "First he tackles Mr. Peterson, and starts ripping, or chopping, him all to pieces." Decker pantomimed switching his focus from Bill's body to the second victim in the hallway. "Then he spots our second vic," he struggled only a second to recall the woman's name from the manifest, "Charlotte Hettersfield, in the hallway. Charlotte turns to run, but he runs her down like a Mack truck. In the narrow corridor, he slams her violently back and forth against the walls and ceiling."

"Okay then, if that's the case, where's the rest of Charlotte's body?" Vickers asked. "So far we only found her face and arm."

Decker bit his lower lip. "I don't know yet. May have taken her body with him."

Sgt. Jenkins then asked, "Then he went down the stairwell and killed the people on the first floor?"

"Nope. Whatever attacked these people didn't use the stairs." When Decker saw everyone waiting for him to explain, he asked them, "Did any of you see blood on the stairs when you came up? Cause I sure didn't. Whatever chased that poor intern down the corridor could barely fit through it, yet the doorframe to the stairwell is just fine."

"Then how'd he move back and forth between floors?" Kate asked, wiping the last of the vomit from her mouth with a paper towel and now caught up in the speculation.

"I don't know yet."

Sgt. Jenkins suddenly offered, "Maybe he jumped back out the hole here, circled around, and attacked the remaining victims on the first floor near the entrance."

Decker shook his head. He was about to say something, but then thought better of it and kept it to himself.

Kate found herself wondering if there was someone in the room he didn't trust. *Is it me?*

"Dex," Vickers asked, "You seem to doubt this was an animal attack."

"I didn't say it wasn't. But I've worked all over Alaska for nearly twenty years, and I've never heard of any polar bear doing anything even remotely like this."

Sergeant Jenkins spoke up from behind. "And I saw holes like that in Afghanistan made from rocket launchers."

Decker nodded. "Yeah, I was thinking the same thing." Turning towards the Sergeant he said, "But the problem with that theory is I didn't see any scorch marks. Did you?"

Sgt. Jenkins glanced back down the hallway for a moment. "No, but the burns could have been blasted off by the wind. It's gotta be blowing at least seventy miles an hour out there."

Kate turned towards Vickers and asked, "Wow. That can actually happen?"

Vickers nodded.

For the first time since they entered the second floor, Grimm lowered his camera. "Wait. Are you telling me you don't think this was some crazy polar bear attack?"

Decker was scanning the room with his flashlight when he answered. "For the sake of argument, let's say it wasn't a polar bear, and someone staged these elaborate deaths to make us think it was a ferocious animal attack."

Kate wasn't buying into Decker's theory. "You really think somebody could have faked all these attacks?" she asked incredulously. "How do you explain the bars bent backwards outside? No human being could've done that."

"Sure he could," Sgt. Jenkins answered for him. "Back home we used to pull tree stumps out of the ground with our pickups and chains all the time."

At this Grimm mumbled, "Why doesn't that surprise me." When he saw the Sergeant glaring menacingly at him, he closed his thin lips. Tightly.

The Sergeant continued, "All I'm saying is the utility winch on our snow tractors could easily bend those bars."

Kate crossed her arms over her chest. With more ferocity than she intended, she said, "Well the pickup truck and winch theory doesn't explain how a woman got pressed up into the ceiling."

"Could've been done with a hydraulic lift or a jury-rigged counterweight system," Decker responded almost immediately.

For reasons she couldn't explain, Kate found her blood boiling. "Boy, you've got an answer for everything, don't you, Detective?"

Decker dropped his eyes to floor. He smiled gently at her, and wore a sad expression. He seemed to be making up his mind about something. Finally, he began, "When I was a kid I couldn't get enough of unexplained mysteries. You know, mythical creatures, Stonehenge, UFOs, things like that," As he listed each one he waved his hands in front of him for dramatic effect. "But the older I got, I learned ... everybody learned the cold hard truth. That infamous photo of the Loch Ness Monster?" When everyone looked at him with raised eyebrows, he continued, "It was a movie prop built by a film crew shooting in the area at the time. The budget for their movie got canceled. So, as a joke, the director photographed their prop and gave the picture to a local dentist to lend it some credibility. Meanwhile it turns out the dentist was quite the practical joker himself. And the film footage of Bigfoot? A rancher confessed on his deathbed it was his buddy in an overstuffed monkey suit. The rancher even told eyewitnesses where they buried the costume. Crop circles? A couple of jokesters flying all over the country using a weighted wooden plank, some rope, and basic geometry. The whole world, including me, believed these wonderful phenomena existed. We wanted to believe in them because we wanted to believe there was still some magic left in the world. But then we learned there is no magic, only some guy behind the curtain pulling everyone's strings."

After a full minute, Vickers was the first one to speak. "Yeah, but Dex, all of those examples are supernatural in nature. We're talking about a polar bear here."

Decker fell silent for a moment. "My point is, any one of these deaths could have been made to appear like some rogue polar bear gone bad, but we've never seen any animal behavior like this in the Arctic before. It's simply unprecedented."

"So ergo, it's gotta be a fake," the Sergeant finished for him.

It was a nice speech, and Kate was surprised the seemingly closed and guarded detective would open up about his childhood, but Kate still wasn't buying into his theory. "Why? Why would someone do that?" she asked.

"Why? For the oldest reason in the book, Kate. To get away with murder."

Vickers wasn't entirely convinced of Decker's hoax theory either. "If that's the case, why would someone want to murder a bunch of scientists way out here on the polar ice cap? I mean, what could possibly be their motive?"

Decker turned his head toward her. "That, Detective Vickers, is exactly what we are here to find out."

Chapter 8

Alonzo and Barton

Why do I always *get paired up with the knuckleheads?*

Mike Barton was getting tired of getting kicked around. He had gotten kicked around for twenty-three years as a gate guard in the Air Force, he had gotten kicked around by his three ex-wives, and now here he was taking the same crap on a different day of his so-called life. He was the one who had leadership experience; he was the one who should be giving orders, and not that country bumpkin from Alabama. Instead he was out here in the freezing cold, trudging through the snow and fueling up the generator in the maintenance shed.

A lackey-boy.

How had it come down to this? Scrimping and saving for twenty-five years, he had finally had enough for ten acres of premium woods in the valley complete with fishing boat, four-wheeler and Harley. But now, wife number three had everything but the bike. While she was enjoying his ten-acre horse ranch with her new divorce lawyer boyfriend, he was living in squalor in a trailer park on the slummy side of Anchorage. He hated Anchorage.

And despite all those years of working and saving, here he was, fifty-fricking-four years old and working as a damn security guard. And to add insult to injury, he had to listen to his knucklehead partner prattle on about comic books, sci-fi movies, and other such nonsense.

I oughtta end it right here. Just put my gun to my head and end it right now. But first I should probably do the world a favor and put a bullet in Sir-Yaps-A-Lot's brain.

Unaware of Barton's thoughts, Alonzo trudged along amiably in the snow beside him. The kid's lips were rarely in the unflapping mode. "Man, can you believe that crap?" Alonzo was yelling above the maniacal shrieks of the wind. "What do you think killed those scientists? I mean, to bend those bars back like that, I mean, shoot, it's gotta be like Nikko said, a polar bear or sumthin'."

And to think, on paper, this kid is considered my equal. In the past he had tried ignoring him, but the kid just went right along yammering, just begging for that bullet.

"Hey, Barton. C'mere man, check this out."

When Barton turned back, he was surprised to find Alonzo no longer keeping pace next to him. Instead, the dope had broken off and was staring at a hole in the ice near the dock.

It was easy to forget they were actually on an island that was off the mainland by a good thirty miles or so. Barton had been on boats out to the island many times in the summer. So he knew for a fact the water was deep enough for large boats to dock. But this time of year, the ice had to go down at least ten to twelve feet.

This was why the hole in the ice, one that was about the width of a small car and went all the way down to the water, gave him pause. But he was damned if he was going to let that idiot Alonzo know that. So instead he yelled to the kid, "Ocean water, so what?"

"You don't think that's weird? I mean, this should all be solid ice. Do you think maybe the scientists made this hole, maybe dropped something down there?" Giving it some more thought, Alonzo added, "Maybe we should tell the detective?"

Barton grouched, "Tell him about what? About a damn hole in the ice? I don't friggin' think so. Probably just a buncha seals or walruses coming and going to the island. Let's just get inside and get this over with." Barton yanked open the door to the maintenance shed, but it was stuck firm. When he glanced back over his shoulder, Alonzo was still peering down into the watery hole.

"Hey man, I think there's something down there, man. Like a whale or something?"

Barton was losing his patience, and was taking his frustration out on the stupid, stupid, frozen-shut door. As he tugged on it over and over, he grunted, "Would you get the hell away from that hole and give me a hand with this damn thing."

Alonzo took one last glimpse down into the pool. He could see the water rippling on the water's surface, but nothing was forthcoming. He then joined Barton over at the shed.

While Barton put his hands on his knees to catch his breath, Alonzo shouldered past him with a "Here, let me try." And with one hand he yanked the door open. "There you go," he said, smiling that imbecilic grin of his.

Barton pushed past him and spat. "Yeah, only because I loosened it up for ya."

The inside of the shed was little more than a concrete bunker with a tin roof. There was a state-of-the-art generator against one wall with a dozen metallic black barrels stacked next to it. Barton immediately identified the problem. The hose that fed the generator was attached to a fuel barrel whose indicator read a big fat zero.

Alonzo entered the shed behind him, talking as usual. "This is like in that horror movie where the monster from outer space picks off the scientists in Antarctica one-by-one. Man, I loved that movie."

Ignoring him, Barton groaned, "Just help me move this thing."

Alonzo continued his jabber-jawing about some movie starring Kurt Russell while they rolled the empty barrel out of the way and hooked up a fresh barrel.

"But you better watch out, man, cause in this movie, I'm the plucky hero while you're the extra who gets snatched up in the jaws of the monster."

Shaking his head in annoyance, Barton finished hooking up the hose to the full fuel barrel. He took off one glove and placed a thumb on the generator's red auto-start button. Holding it there he told Alonzo, "Radio that idiot Jenkins that I'm getting ready to throw the switch."

"What? Oh, yeah, right, man."

Barton watched with disdain while Alonzo first tried to grab his radio off his belt with his gloves on. Then, after realizing that wasn't going to work, the moron finally removed his gloves and pulled out his radio. "Sgt. Jenkins for Alonzo, come in, over." When he was greeted only with static, he tried again, and again, and again.

Geez, how long will it take dumbass here to realize his radio won't work in this concrete bunker? "Why don't you try your radio outside?" Barton asked sardonically.

Alonzo missed the sarcasm and was about to try a fourth time but then responded, "Oh yeah, right. Probably too much interference in here with the concrete and all, huh?"

Barton smiled stiffly and only nodded. *You think? You friggin' moron.*

When Alonzo stepped outside, he left the door open so the snow could blow in.

Well, I'm sure as hell not going to dig that snow out so we can shut the door. Instead, Barton continued to man the switch while he waited for confirmation from Alonzo. Losing patience by the second, he yelled, "Alonzo! Alonzo, did you radio them or not?"

"Screw this crap," he mumbled. "I'm not freezing my ass off out here anymore while they're all nice and warm and toasty inside." And without waiting to hear from Alonzo, he threw the switch. The heavy-duty generator thundered to life, and Barton choked on the fumes as the air flooded with diesel fuel. With any luck, the Sarge had his fork in the toaster when the power came on. An image of the Sarge getting electrocuted with those ridiculous bottle-cap glasses of his caused Barton to chuckle.

After putting his glove back on, Barton ventured outside. Against his better judgment, he turned and, with a few angry shoves and curses at Alonzo for carelessly leaving it open, he managed to slam the door closed. Still facing the door, he thought for the briefest of moments he heard a heavy splash.

Barton trudged his way through the snow towards the hole Alonzo had pointed out earlier. Sure enough, Alonzo's tracks went right towards the watery opening. *But where the hell was he?* He stomped over to the edge, reminding himself not to be a hero and fall in too. But he had to at least be able to tell everyone he had tried to save the kid.

Barton went as close to the edge as he dared. Careful not to slip on the ice, he leaned over and peered down into the depths. Sure enough, he could see air bubbles frothing at the water where the kid must have slipped off the ice and gone straight down.

What a dumbass. Clothes must've weighted him down and taken him straight to the bottom. Wait till I tell the guys back at the camp.

Barton reached for his radio. Before calling in about Alonzo's mishap, he gazed down into the water to check for his partner one last time. In those last few seconds of his life, Barton saw an explosion of water coming towards his face, barely glimpsing the jagged teeth closing in on both sides of his head.

Chapter 9

Arctodus Simus

Kate shivered every time someone found another piece of human carnage.

For several hours, Decker and his team of criminologists photographed, bagged, and tagged nearly all the scientists' remains. A leg here, a finger there, an eyeball found in a sink downstairs.

It was slow going.

At the moment the lights came back on, Grimm was using metallic tongs from his evidence collection kit to pick up a human hand severed at the wrist. It had a gold wedding band on the ring finger. With an odd detachment, he examined it for a moment, and then placed the appendage in a yellow plastic bag. The hand had been found on the first floor, and they theorized that it belonged to the research assistant, Sanjay Patel, because it wasn't big enough to belong to Bill the engineer, nor white enough to belong to Eugene Banks.

Seeing her looking over at him, he exclaimed half-heartedly, "Yay, we got the power back on."

Through process of elimination of the human pieces, all but Eugene Banks had been identified as found remains. Thus far Decker had concluded that Bill Peterson and Charlotte Hettersfield had been killed upstairs, and Project Manager Sierra Banks and research assistant Sanjay Patel slaughtered downstairs near the main entrance.

Now that the lights were back on, bloody oversized paw prints were visible everywhere, on the floors, on the walls, and on the pantry doors. To Kate, more and more it was looking like an unfortunate and horrific animal attack, but even with the blaringly obvious bear tracks, Decker still did not seem convinced that the whole thing wasn't a hoax and insisted that Vickers dust for prints. She and Sgt. Jenkins had also been printed for comparisons to rule them out.

Back on the first floor, Vickers was hunched over one of the more distinctive bear tracks in the dried blood on the floor when she said aloud, "Hey, boss. Come take a look at this."

It was the tone in her voice that worried Kate the most. She sounded scared. And Detective Vickers didn't really seem like the type to scare easily.

Kate watched as Vickers flashed a photograph of the bloody paw print, then dropped a white numbered placard next to it and photographed it a second time. It was a time-consuming procedure that Kate had become familiar with over the last several hours. Unlike in the television shows or movies, real crime scene investigators didn't just pick up evidence the moment they found it and hold it up for the audience to see. Instead, genuine investigators would photograph found evidence where it lay, then put a placard next to it, photograph it again, and then plot its location on a scale diagram, sometimes on a notebook, other times on some form of electronic device. Finally, with gloved hands, they would place the evidence in a plastic evidence bag and label it.

As she and Detective Decker joined her, Vickers asked Decker, "Did you notice anything strange about these bear tracks right here?"

Decker knelt down next to Vickers and examined the tracks. "They appear to be more bear tracks all right. Just like the others."

Vickers nodded. Then, turning towards the Sergeant, tagging and bagging nearby, she began, "Sgt. Jenkins, you strike me as the hunter type …"

Jenkins zipped another evidence bag closed and grinned back at her broadly. "I've bagged my share of moose now and again."

"More than your share would be my guess," Decker responded.

"Hey, for the last time, that was self-defense," the Sergeant retorted. "Besides, that moose was in my yard."

Ignoring them both, Vickers asked, "And you've lived in Alaska for some time now. Do these bear tracks seem uncommonly large for a bear?"

Jenkins came over, bent over the tracks with his hands on his knees and gazed at them intently. Increasing his normal country twang, as he often did when he felt the moment warranted it, he responded, "Well, Ma'am, them's bout the biggest damn bear tracks I have ever seen." He pointed to the width. "I mean, judging by the width of its track, I estimate its height to be at least fifteen feet tall on the hind legs. I ain't never seen anything that big before, not even up here in the Arctic."

"I seriously doubt you will see a bear track that size anywhere in the world," Decker added.

"Maybe it's the Yeti," the Sergeant joked.

This got a grin from Decker and Vickers, but Kate wasn't so sure it wasn't the Yeti.

What else could have bent those bars back like that?

"Don't be ridiculous," Grimm said, joining them. "The Yeti is indigenous to the Himalayas, not the Arctic Circle."

Kate wasn't sure if Grimm was kidding or not. The criminologist was kind of hard to figure out.

Vickers frowned at Grimm. "That ... that's what you keyed up on? The Yeti's origins?"

Grimm shrugged his shoulders. "Hey, keep an open mind, remember. We need to consider all possibilities." Then Grimm stared at the track again and tilted his head like a dog trying to watch TV. "You know, actually, I have seen a track like that before." When everyone turned towards him, he realized he was the focus of attention. The greasy scientist drank this in for a moment and then said, "*Arctodus simus*, more commonly referred to as the short-faced bear." Grimm took out a pen and pointed at the track for emphasis. "You see here? Not only the immense size of the paw, but another important difference from our North American bears is that rather than being pigeon toed and having a waddling gait, *A. simus* had toes extending straight forward, presumably enabling them to move much faster than its modern descendants."

"Anything else?" Decker asked dryly, but Grimm must have missed the sarcasm because the skinny scientist continued, enthralled by this fresh track of a creature thought to be extinct long ago.

"Short-faced bears were the largest carnivores in North America during the Ice Age. Unusually tall and carnivorous. The largest known specimens stood over fourteen feet when upright."

"What?" Kate exclaimed, "That's four feet higher than a basketball hoop!" She suddenly found herself wondering where the Sergeant kept his shotgun and why he wasn't carrying it right now.

Seeing her concern, Grimm grinned. "Yep. The largest carnivorous animal to walk the earth since the age of the dinosaurs."

"How much did they weigh?" Vickers asked.

"Purely speculation, of course, but if memory serves there was a calculation of the autumn weight of a giant short-faced bear. Considering it had its full component of fat, based on the diameter of the upper hind leg, it would have weighed approximately a ton-and-a-half, about three thousand pounds."

"Is ... is that a lot for a bear?" Kate asked nervously.

"Immense," Decker intoned. "That's about one ton heavier than the largest polar bear in recorded history."

Grimm's tone was grave. "Beringia was truly a land of Ice Age monsters. The biggest grazers and their most fearsome predators were far larger than any mammals that live on the continent today."

"And where does our short-faced bear rank amongst them?" Vickers asked, moving her elbow to rest on her sidearm as if to casually confirm it was still there.

Still recording on his digital camera, Grimm said, "*A. simus* was the largest, most efficient killing machine among the Pleistocene land mammals of North America. It could run over forty kilometers an hour and could strike with enough force to kill a fully grown elephant with one blow. It preyed on large herbivores, such as bison muskoxen, caribou, deer, horses, and ground sloths. In short, this guy feared nothing."

Seeing Kate's growing concern, Vickers clearly had had enough of Grimm's fearmongering. "But this scenario is impossible; I thought *Arctodus simus* died out with the rest of the Ice Age animals toward the close of the last glaciations, about ten thousand years ago."

Grimm lowered his camera and frowned. "Why impossible? Yes, most Ice Age animals did die about ten thousand years ago, but isolated populations of wooly mammoths were discovered on Wrangell Island and believed to have existed as recently as four thousand years ago."

Sgt. Jenkins frowned, and said "Four thousand years is a long way from the here and now."

Grimm sighed, and without so much as glancing back at the sergeant he said, "Yes, that is true. But in 1920, a French explorer reported seeing one in a remote area of Siberia. And as recently as the late 1990s, mammoth carcasses were found in the area with meat still on the bones."

While everyone thought about the existence of such a terrifying creature, Kate found herself backing away from the group before she realized she was even doing it. She needed some space, some time to think. She hadn't signed up for this. Everyone was dead, and now Grimm was saying there was a giant-sized prehistoric bear on the loose.

When she had first found out about the murders, she had hoped to salvage any research she could. But under these horrific circumstances, no one could blame her for getting on the first plane back to Anchorage. How could they? How could she save anything when she couldn't even save herself?

Chapter 10

Now Entering Phase III

Around supper time, adrenaline had robbed everyone of their energy, and the five of them had gathered in the kitchen for a much-needed break. Everyone was there except Nikko and the other two guards, who were outside keeping watch and the tractors fully fueled.

Vickers had brought enough protein bars for everyone, but Decker had decided it was okay to raid the refrigerator under these dire and unusual circumstances.

"Now do you believe this was a bear attack?" Kate asked Decker, chowing down on one of the delicious omelets the Sergeant prepared for everyone. Vickers didn't glance up from her own plate of eggs, but she could tell everyone was waiting to hear his answer, as was she.

Detective Decker sank back in his seat, studied them all for a moment, as though deciding something, then began to speak. As usual, he did not disappoint. "State of California, September 1981, in the Sierra Nevada Mountains near Collins Lake recreation area. Some kids claimed they found Bigfoot's tracks near the lake's edge across from the campground area. Experts flew in from all over the world, photographs were taken, mortar casts were made, and even animal biologists testified the tracks could have only been made by the mythical creature Bigfoot." Decker took a bite of an apple with a resounding crunch.

Kate shook her head. "Let me guess, two guys in gorilla suits?"

"No, worse. A little ol' woman made giant feet out of plaster and mortar. Stuck little wooden poles in them and would tread through the snow with her homemade Bigfoot contraption like a cross-country skier."

"Yeah, but wouldn't observers have seen her tracks too?" Vickers asked, from the other side of the table.

Decker flashed a knowing smile. "They would if the woman wasn't ingenious enough to back up in her own tracks and erase them from existence with pine needles, leaving only the Bigfoot tracks."

"That's an old Indian trick right there," the Sergeant interjected. He was still wearing an apron that read Kiss the Cook, and whisking up something that appeared to be cake batter in a metallic bowl.

Vickers sighed, rubbed her forehead, and asked, "And this little old lady, she did this, why?"

"You mean, what was her motive?" Decker asked.

Vickers raised her eyebrows impatiently and nodded, annoyed. "Uh-huh."

Decker grinned broadly. "Because she was a widow, and the only thing she had left to her name when her husband died was his camping cabins. As you can imagine, after the Bigfoot sighting, business was booming for the next several months. She sold the cabins at an enormous profit and moved down to Florida."

Kate took a bite of her toast. Vickers had suggested that it might settle her stomach. She should have chewed cautiously, but she found herself so hungry.

Grimm stared at Decker in disbelief. "Where's your sense of wonder? Didn't you ever watch *Twilight Zone*, or *In Search of...* as a kid?"

For the briefest of seconds, Decker's face lit up like a little boy's. "Are you kidding? I loved those shows. Especially *Twilight Zone*. I used to set my alarm to wake me up at 11:50 p.m. because it always came on at midnight." But then as he thought about it for a few seconds, his normal countenance resumed. "But those shows are fiction," he said, rising from the table with his empty plate. "These days I'm more of a *60 Minutes* kind of guy."

As he went back to the kitchen, Kate found herself wondering, *What happened to him that made him so cynical?*

When he returned with some orange juice he said, "Look, I'm not saying it wasn't a polar bear attack. There's certainly enough evidence to support that theory. But what's more plausible? That someone has a motive to fake a polar bear attack, or that a giant prehistoric bear has magically arisen from a four-thousand-year-long slumber and returned from the Ice Age?"

Vickers was the first to speak. "Okay, so if this is all some kind of sick and crazy hoax, what kind of motive are we talking about here, Dex?"

"I don't know yet. Maybe the scientists found an oil deposit or something."

To Kate, that seemed like a logical possibility.

Sgt. Jenkins stopped his mad whisking for a moment and added, "Yeah, an oil strike could be worth billions to an oil company, especially with such a nice usable landmass for a base platform. People have killed a lot more for a lot less."

Decker shrugged. "And with Alaskan oil pipeline falling below nine hundred thousand barrels per day, there is definitely motive to find a new well."

"Ya know, the Arctic also hosts a variety of mining activity," Grimm said. "Could be minerals, precious metals, maybe?"

Kate was beginning to believe Decker's theory. And it seemed everyone else was beginning to also. Was it really so implausible? *What's the cost of a few movie special effects to frame a polar bear for murder when you're talking about billions of dollars a day?*

Then Vickers voiced what they were all thinking. "So your working theory is someone wanted to run the scientists off and claim the island for themselves."

Decker nodded.

Grimm hesitated before forking in another heaping bite. "Sounds like we got ourselves a regular *Scooby Doo* mystery on our hands."

Decker regarded the nerdy scientist with a slight grin. "If all of this really is an elaborate hoax, we just need to find the motive for the murders; then the evidence will present itself."

Kate was starting to feel safer as Decker's hoax theory became more plausible, but then Sgt. Jenkins asked, "Yeah, but Dex, I hate to shoot Cheerios in your theory, but if you're going to frame a bear, why would you use paw prints that belonged to an oversized prehistoric monster?"

Decker was silent for a moment before answering. "Yeah, I'd given some thought about that, too. Maybe it was a museum piece and it was all they had on hand?"

Even for Decker that was a reach. The brief jovial mood of the group started to drift away again.

Without gazing up from her cup of hot green tea cooling in her cupped hands, Vickers asked, "Just a hypothetical. What if we really are dealing with some kind of prehistoric throwback here?"

Decker frowned while he considered the possibility. He must've been lost in thought for a moment because he seemed surprised to find everyone waiting for an answer. "I'll tell you what, if we haven't found out anything more to support my hoax theory in the next hour, I say we pack up our gear and the evidence we collected, and get the hell out of here. We can always come back with a polar bear expert, Fish and Game, and a lot more firepower."

"I hear that," Grimm said in a tone about as enthusiastic as Kate had ever heard him.

Vickers slid from her seat, and under her breath she said, "Sounds like a good plan to me."

Before they all could break off, everyone jumped when Nikko threw his gearbag roughly on the kitchen counter. Kate wasn't sure, but she thought she had seen Decker's hand move quickly to his holster.

Oblivious to everyone's nervousness, Nikko brushed snow off his shoulders onto the kitchen counter and floor. And when he threw his hood back he shook more snow out of his unkempt jet black hair.

He unclipped his radio and sat it on the counter. "Well, it's official. I barely got through to the mainland before communications went out completely. We are officially in Condition Phase III."

"Phase III," Decker repeated, in a low voice. "Any idea for how long?"

Nikko shouldered his way out of his heavy coat, oblivious to all the snow he was leaving on the floor. "I don't know, could be days. Weeks even. Depends on the storm."

"What's that mean?" Kate asked no one in particular.

Decker must've seen the worried look on her face. "Don't worry; it's not uncommon up here for this time of year."

But Kate didn't want to be placated; she wanted to be educated. "Yeah, thank you, Mr. Almanac, but what I want to know is what do the different phase conditions mean?"

Sgt. Jenkins responded in military fashion, "Phase I, normal winter hazardous conditions. Let people know where you're going and when you arrive. Prepare for the worst and hope for the best. Phase II, normal travel is strictly prohibited without special authorization, and even then all personnel travel only in convoys and escorted by Security Arctic survival-trained officers."

"And Phase III?" Kate asked.

Decker responded for the Sergeant, his tone more serious. "In Phase III you stop what you're doing and you stay put. No one goes anywhere or gets in or out."

Kate felt her heart sink and her breakfast rise. "So what does Phase III mean to us?"

Sgt. Jenkins removed his hat, and then replaced it. He blinked at her from behind those bottle-cap glasses of his. "Well, Ma'am, that's an easy one. Whether we like it or not, it means we're stuck out here."

Chapter 11

Dig Site

To keep her mind off the fact that they were trapped inside a remote facility filled with dead bodies on an island surrounded by crushing pack ice, with either a sadistic killer or prehistoric bear on the loose (take your pick), Kate went back downstairs intent upon salvaging whatever research she could.

Where to begin?

The first floor remained an utter mess. Up until now, everything had been off limits. Sgt. Jenkins and Nikko had been kind enough to mop up any remaining blood, but the tables and chairs were still overturned, and printouts lay everywhere. At least with main power back on, she could now see what she was looking at.

As she was picking up loose printouts and stacking them in her hand, she realized that many of the file folders marked DIG SITE were empty. In fact, the more she searched, the more empty file folders she began to find.

Kate wasn't sure what to believe anymore, but in lieu of the missing files, she was starting to believe Decker's theory, and she was starting to form one of her own. One thing was for certain; someone had obviously ransacked their research.

In her orientation binder, she remembered something about a fire safe hidden in a locker cabinet. After retrieving her gear bag from where she had left it in her quarters, she removed the binder. Using the binder's map as a guide, she soon found the safe. The mini vault was hidden behind an ordinary cabinet. The only problem was that the combination was not written down in the binder. She glanced around for anywhere it might be written down but didn't see any of the usual suspects: a sticky note taped nearby, writing on the wall or the ceiling.

Darn, and so close too.

Kate thought about asking the detectives to break into the safe, but there were two problems: first the safe appeared formidable, and second, whatever was inside, they'd confiscate as evidence.

On Sierra's computer, a plastic lucky charm grinned mockingly at Kate. It was a caricature of a polar bear holding a broken wooden sign that read, "Gone Fishin'." Kate smiled for a moment as happy memories of working with Eugene and Sierra flooded back into her mind, until she was reminded of the fact she'd never see either of them again.

In another lifetime, they would've been better friends, but Sierra always put her work first and even her husband was barely lucky enough to get any free time she allowed herself. As she gazed at the charm, lost in happy memories, a spark of realization hit her. Sierra used to write down combinations to her computer on the bottom of that stupid bear.

Kate tentatively stretched out her hand and lifted the lucky charm bear from its perch and, after checking to make sure no one was watching, peered underneath. Sure enough, there it was, an eight-digit combination.

A few minutes later and she was in the safe.

Much to her disappointment, there was nothing inside. Whoever had ransacked the files had gotten away with whatever was in the safe.

Then another thought popped into her head. Thus far, the only body the detectives had not found was Eugene Banks, Sierra's husband. And he would know where Sierra kept the combination, just as she did. Was Banks somehow involved with the murders? Kate found the idea extremely implausible. Banks worshiped the ground Sierra walked on. He could never do anything to hurt her, or anyone else, could he...?

Frowning, she closed the safe.

As she began tidying up the lab again, Kate spied Sierra's infamous grease board on squeaky wheels lying on the floor. Another fond memory: Sierra used to use the old grease board in her classroom to sum up her findings. Most people today used computer applications with special effects. But Sierra believed her work, not nifty presentations, would speak for itself, which it always did.

She picked up the grease board and was surprised to find nothing written on it. *Huh, that's odd. That doesn't seem like Sierra at all. Maybe on the other side?* Kate flipped the grease board over. Then and there, out in the open for anyone to see, was a photograph taped in the center. Staring at the photograph, Kate now understood why her mysterious benefactors had attached her to this project. The photograph was the sole reason why she in particular had been chosen and sent to this miserable place.

The photo was an image of a partially excavated dig site inside a glaciated cavern. Kate could see a roof of ice overhead, and the walls were also solid blue ice. Kate could see roughhewn blocks of stone submerged in the ice like some kind of pre-Neolithic temple. Then, staring more intently at the photo, she saw a partially unearthed jade totem pole. She recalled her last symposium, specifically the missing Chinese expedition who had discovered an undersea jade totem that vanished after they had transmitted several photos. Although smaller and with slightly different carvings, the totem in the photograph matched the Chinese discovery incredibly.

Kate quickly scanned the notes that surrounded and were connected to the photo by lines like spokes on a bicycle wheel.

One printed report summarized that carbon dating confirmed that the site had been trapped in the glacier and undisturbed for at least ten thousand years. Kate examined the photo of the dig site again. She wasn't positive, but it appeared that some of the excavated blocks had little black markings on them. *Could those be some sort of hieroglyphs?* That would be unprecedented. It confirmed all her own theories about a first people who had migrated from the North. Thoughts of vindication immediately sprang to mind.

Where is it located?

Kate had to see the dig site for herself. All thoughts of imminent danger were forgotten.

Also taped to the grease board was a simply drawn but accurate map of Dead Bear Island. She had forgotten that was the name of their location.

She delicately, almost reverently touched the photo. "Banks," she muttered aloud. Sierra's husband was always doodling, and drawing maps was one of his favorite pastimes. A twinge of sadness came over her, but she fought it off with the fact that they still hadn't found his body yet. Maybe he was at the dig site. Maybe, just maybe Banks was still alive.

In Banks's sketch, the island was shaped like a horseshoe, slightly canted at the bottom to the left. Using the facility as a reference, she saw that the dig site lay clear on the other side of the island near the southeast dock. Spotting the drawings labeled as DOCKS, she was reminded that in the summer the island was surrounded by water, not pack ice. Sierra and Banks must've reached the opposite end of the horseshoe-shaped island by boat.

Above the drawing, Banks had drawn a rusted-out cargo ship beached on the northeast end of the island. A string of yarn connected the drawing to a photo of a similar ship that appeared to have beached long ago.

Okay, that's nice, Banks, you found an old cargo ship, but how do I get to the dig site?

Checking Banks's hastily drawn map again, she traced a land route through a giant graveyard on the beach near the island's center. Another string ran off the hand drawn map and connected to another photo. This one was an old black and white photograph of a whalebone graveyard. The antiquated photograph showed Eskimos, or more appropriately named Inupiaqs, carving up meat amongst piles of what Banks had correctly identified as mammoth bones. The year 1915 was written in the lower right hand corner of the photo.

So did the natives find a nearly intact wooly mammoth preserved in the ice? Of course, the loss of the find was monumental, but even she could not help but wonder what wooly mammoth tasted like.

Kate returned to Banks's map and started tracing the route again to the dig site. It appeared that after passing through the whalebone graveyard, one reached the bottom of a cliff side that was permanently frozen. Moving past two crumbling stelae, or so Sierra's notes indicated, was an entrance to what was clearly a manmade tunnel. Once there, Banks's drawing showed the tunnel went down through the glacial ice at a steep angle and into a cavern.

Kate stared at the photo of the dig site again. The jade totem pole alone would be worth millions. No. It would be beyond millions, or even billions. A find like this would be priceless.

And then the realization began to sink in. Detective Decker might be completely right after all. A treasured artifact like the jade totem would be worth the kind of hoax he was suggesting. Drive the scientists away, keep it a secret, and claim the site, and everything in it, for yourself.

That's when she knew that she had found Decker's missing motive.

Chapter 12

Phase III

Kate was faced with a difficult decision.

Should I tell Decker?

At first she couldn't wait to tell him about what she had found, but now the excitement yielded to caution. She thought it might be best to keep the dig site a secret and tell only her employer. If word got out that the jade totem really existed, she'd have to deal with grave robbers, treasure hunters, and other competing researchers. And the local natives might sue for ownership.

When she had come back upstairs, she had had every intention of telling Detective Decker about the dig site despite her misgivings, but when she walked in to the rec room she was surprised to see the crime scene was now turned into a construction zone. For starters, Sgt. Jenkins and Detective Decker had already taken away the ping pong table and other pieces of plywood and used them to patch up the damaged wall.

Meanwhile, Grimm and Nikko were taping up the windows that were splintered with hurricane tape. And Vickers was in the kitchen with a clipboard and appeared to be inventorying the canned food. Several blue bins sealed with evidence tape were neatly stacked against the wall and nearly all the blood was gone.

"What's going on? I thought you guys were still working on your investigation?"

Vickers gazed up from her clipboard for a moment, studied her face, and then resumed her checklist. "Mission has changed. It's more of a survival situation now than an investigation. Besides, earlier you seemed pretty convinced the culprit was a bear on steroids."

Kate liked Vick. With every fiber of her being, she wanted to blurt out what she had found. But what if the same thing that happened to the Chinese discovery happened here, too? The data might be lost forever. Knowing Vick was waiting for an answer, she said, "I ... I'm starting to think maybe Decker's got a point. Maybe somebody could have faked all of this."

When Vickers chuckled, something Kate had never seen her do, she asked, "What's so funny?"

Vickers scratched her forehead with the cover of her pen. "That's funny, because just a few minutes ago Decker told me that now he thinks you're the one that might be right."

"I didn't realize I had a theory," Kate replied.

"So you didn't think it this was all caused by a giant prehistoric cave bear?"

Kate shrugged. Before she could reply, Decker called over to the Sergeant, "Maybe one more sheet of plywood over the center. What do you think?"

"Sounds right by me," Sgt. Jenkins responded.

As Kate watched Decker lift another piece of heavy plywood and hammer it into place, she mused aloud, "Boy, they sure don't make them like him anymore,"

Vick scrunched her eyebrows but kept working and asked, "You mean Dex?"

When Kate nodded, Vickers added, "That's for sure," and she snapped the pantry lid closed. "You like him, don't you?"

Kate felt her cheeks flush. Even if Vickers was not a trained behavioral signals expert, Kate knew she was busted. There was no use denying it, so she answered, "Well, yeah. I mean, even though he's a little cranky every now and then, he's good-looking, intelligent, and despite the rugged, tough-guy exterior he puts on, you can tell there's this little boy trapped deep inside just dying to get out." As an afterthought, she added under her breath, "Too bad he's married."

"Oh, Decker's not married. At least not anymore."

Damn it if Vickers wasn't waiting and watching for her reaction. While Kate considered Decker's wedding band, Vickers must have read her thoughts because she offered, "His wife died five years ago." Now it was Kate's turn to study the female investigator. Vickers's eyes became vacant, as though reliving some terrible memory. "He still wears the ring, though." When she realized Kate was studying her, she shook it off and said, "It was awful. If Dex didn't have his kids to care for after losing his wife, he probably wouldn't have made it." A smile then crossed her face, as though now reliving some happy memory. "You should have met him before the accident. He was so funny, always made us laugh." Vick's brows furrowed once more. "It was tough on him. It was tough on all of us."

"What happened to his wife?"

Vickers's tone became firm. "No matter what anyone tells you, even Dex, it wasn't his fault." Vickers opened her mouth to speak further but Decker walked towards them.

He didn't appear happy.

Oh, crap. Did he hear us?

"Hey, Kate, have you seen Alonzo or Barton?"

"You mean the two security guards?" she asked, relieved he hadn't heard them talking. Kate thought about it before answering. When was the last time she had seen them? "No, not since we first entered the facility."

Decker frowned. He turned over his shoulder and asked, "How about you Nikko, you seen Alonzo or Barton?"

Nikko, busy taping up the plexiglass windows, answered, "No, sir. Last time I saw them was when they headed for the maintenance shed to get the generator back on."

"You mean they weren't in the tractors with you?" Sgt. Jenkins asked.

Nikko shook his head. "Nope. I thought they were inside here with you guys. They're not upstairs taking a nap or something?"

Decker turned his head towards Vickers and gave her a questioning glance. Before he could ask, she said, "I'll go up and double check, but I was just up there twenty minutes ago and no one was on the third floor."

Sgt. Jenkins, still wearing a tool belt and wielding a hammer, asked, "Want me to suit up and check the shed?"

"Naw. You finish up here. I want to check the exterior of the facility for myself anyway. Besides, you're twice the handyman I am."

"Take the shotgun. It's near the entrance," Sgt. Jenkins said in a voice that was not open for discussion.

"What's it loaded with?"

"The usual arsenal up here: fireworks, bean bags, and slugs."

Decker nodded, but as he turned to leave the Sergeant added, "If what killed those scientists really is a bear, you might not have time for more than one shot. I'd lose the less-than-lethal crap and load it up with slugs only."

"Copy that, and thanks, Mom." Decker patted the Sergeant on the back and headed for the stairwell.

"I'm serious, Dex," the Sergeant shouted after him. "If it's bigger than a person, shoot first and we can identify it later."

For several moments Kate thought about telling Decker what she had found. She finally concluded that it was the right thing to do. She ran down the stairwell after him but by the time she caught up, he was already in the entry pulling on his heavy winter gear.

"Hey, Detective Decker, wait up."

Pulling on his heavy coat, he said gently, "Kate, I've told you, just call me, James."

"Okay," she replied, tucking her hair behind one ear. "James. Listen, I've wanted to tell you about some of the research I found. I think I know ..."

Before she could finish, Grimm abruptly entered the entry and said, "Hey, Dex, mind if I tag along?"

That's weird, I didn't think Grimm was the hero type, Kate thought.

Echoing her thoughts, Decker asked him, "Really?"

As the nerdy technician searched his pockets, he muttered, "Yeah man, I am dying for a smoke."

There it is.

Decker pulled on his gloves and then picked up Sgt. Jenkins's shotgun. He racked the slide and peered into the chamber. His movements were quick and practiced. Satisfied with the ammo in the breech, he racked the weapon closed. He then slipped into the weapon's harness so the weapon hung safely across his chest with the barrel pointing down. "Sorry, Kate; you were about to tell me something?"

Kate glanced to where Grimm was hopping on one leg, trying to pull on his oversized snow pants. Turning back to Decker, she said "It can wait."

Chapter 13

Hypothermic

Decker and Grimm had been gone for nearly an hour now.

Kate knew what everyone was thinking, but so far, no one mentioned it. The storm outside was worsening by the minute. As they approached the hour mark, Sgt. Jenkins couldn't take it anymore and started suiting up in his foul weather gear. As soon as he was dressed, he told everyone to wait for him to get back.

The Sergeant opened the inner door to the entry but fortunately for him, before he could step out the damaged exterior door, Decker and Grimm had returned.

Over the Sergeant's shoulder, Kate could see Detective Decker standing outside in the bear cage. He was half-carrying Grimm off one shoulder.

Sgt. Jenkins backpedaled into the facility and the three of them stumbled through the entry and onto the floor of the main room.

The wind was blowing so hard that it took the combined strength of all three men just to shut the interior hatch. Even in that brief moment, mounds of snow had piled inside.

Both men propped themselves up against the wall. They were so cold that they couldn't undress themselves without help.

"Oh my gosh, you guys are half-frozen," Vickers announced with alarm. She turned to Nikko and commanded, "Nikko, go upstairs to the personnel quarters and fill two tubs with warm water."

"Did you find Alonzo or Barton?" Sgt. Jenkins asked Decker with concern in his voice. Clearly he was feeling responsible for not checking on his men sooner. "Did you see any signs of them?"

Decker was shivering so uncontrollably he could barely manage to say, "No sign of them anywhere. We checked the shed, the tractors; we even circled the facility."

As Vickers and the Sergeant helped Decker get out of his soaked gear, Kate moved over to help Grimm.

Teeth chattering, Grimm said vehemently, "Decker wouldn't let us come back inside until we checked the entire perimeter. I think I passed out. I thought I was a goner." He began to cry and sobbed, "I could have died." A second later, he succumbed to unconsciousness. Kate could literally feel the cold coming off the man's body.

Vickers was all business. She locked eyes with Decker and said "Dex, you're suffering from hypothermia. I want to submerse you and Grimm in some warm water and check you over for frostbite."

"No, no, don't do that," Decker replied feebly. "I'm fine," and then passed out in her arms.

—— <> ——

As well as being a behavioral signals expert, a detective for the Alaska Bureau of Investigations, and a bush pilot, Vickers was also a survival instructor. Under her direction, the others worked in two teams. First they stripped both men down to their skivvies, then carried them upstairs and lowered each into a tub of warm water.

Vickers, also an EMT III, found a first aid kit and hooked up a field IV drip to each man. She then went back and forth between bathrooms monitoring their vitals. Nikko was assigned to watch over Grimm while Kate attended James. Primarily, Kate's job was to keep Decker's head from slipping underwater.

Against Vickers's wishes, Sgt. Jenkins suited up and went back out and searched for his men. Vickers had made the Sergeant promise to at least tie himself off to the outer hatch and to only go outside for ten-minute intervals.

Decker was still fast asleep in the tub and had yet to return to consciousness. Kate did her best to make him comfortable and propped his head up with towels. Decker was much more muscular than she would have imagined, not steroid body builder or anything, but he definitely didn't miss many workouts at the gym. She also saw vicious jagged scars crisscrossing his chest. The tissue damage seemed excessive even for a man in his line of work.

Car accident?

Kate recalled Vickers's words about him losing his wife. Vickers had said it wasn't Decker's fault. Were the two connected somehow?

As the minutes wore on, she studied his firm jaw. There was something peaceful about watching a domesticated lion at rest. She hadn't even realized she was tracing the scars on his chest with her forefinger when Decker said quietly, eyes only half open, "You know, usually a girl buys me dinner first."

Startled, Kate jumped to her feet so fast she sent the IV bag splashing into the bath water. Angry, she asked, "How long have you been awake?"

In spite of his condition, Decker replied with a sleepy grin, "Long enough to see you massaging my chest."

"I did no such thing," Kate stammered. "I was ... I mean to say ..."

"Hey, look who's awake." It was Vickers. She was standing in the bathroom doorway and leaning on the frame with her arms crossed.

Great, just great. She probably saw me too. What was I thinking?

Vickers moved over to the tub and knelt next to him. Speaking to Decker she asked, "How do you feel, Dex?"

Groggily he answered, "I'm fine. Why? How are you?" Then glancing down at his half naked body, he said to her, "Any excuse to get my shirt off."

"You wish," Vick replied, splashing him and then they both laughed. Kate found herself wondering what kind of relationship the two of them shared, and if it was more than just being longtime partners. Then in a voice nearly choking back tears Vicks said, "You really had me worried, you stupid jerk."

"Naw, I'm fine. Nothing compared to that time we worked that case with the naked guy in HavenPort. Remember that?"

Vickers started to say something, sniffed loudly, wiped away her tears and then began again. "Yeah, you nearly drowned."

Kate retreated to the doorway, was about to say something, and realized there was nothing more to say.

She stepped out of the bathroom, eased the door shut and found herself in the hallway, alone once more.

Chapter 14

Night-Night

By the time they had gotten Decker and Grimm out of their respective bathtubs and amongst the living, it was near midnight.

Vickers suggested they all get some sleep while she and Sgt. Jenkins took first watch. Decker agreed only upon the condition they would wake him in four hours to relieve them. They had put Grimm by himself in the engineer's room and helped Decker into the project manager's bedroom, which was big by remote research facility standards.

"Knock, knock," Kate said gently, easing the door open quietly with her foot. She was carrying a pitcher of water and a glass, being careful not to wake him if he was already out.

When she entered the room the light over his bed stand was still on but Decker was fast asleep. The room was warm enough that he was uncovered. She also saw that he held his cell phone loosely in one hand dangling precariously off the bed.

That's crazy; who's he trying to call? You can barely get a signal on the mainland, let alone way the heck out here on the pack ice.

As she moved closer to his bedside, she realized that Decker hadn't been trying to make a call. He had been looking at pictures on his camera phone.

Kate put the pitcher and glass down on the nightstand. She had only intended to place the phone there, too, but she couldn't help glancing at the photo on the display. It was a photo of two cute children, a boy about four and a six-year-old girl, wrapped up in each other's arms and smiling back at the camera.

Kate felt herself blink in the light.

She lightly placed the cell phone on the night table and when she started toward the exit she heard Decker say, "That's my two little ones, Sam and Alexandria."

Kate only jumped slightly this time and said, "I didn't mean to wake you. Vickers thought you might be thirsty and asked me to bring you some water before turning in for bed."

It only occurred to Kate now that Vickers might be trying to set them up.

Decker rolled his eyes and smiled, as if realizing some joke she wasn't in on. Then he smiled at her. "Thanks."

"Sure," Kate replied. After a moment of awkward silence, she glanced at the photo on his phone again and heard herself say, "Your kids are crazy adorable."

"Alexandria is seven, going on thirty," Decker explained, gazing on the photo longingly. "And strong, sweet, and silent Sam will be five next month."

Kate only nodded. Decker didn't volunteer anything about his dead wife, and she chose not to push him about her, or how it happened. She remembered Vickers's words though, about her death not being Decker's fault, "no matter what anyone tells you."

"What about you?" Decker asked, interrupting her thoughts. "You have any kids?"

Kate shook her head a little sadly. "No. You could fit my love life on the back of a postage stamp and still have room left over."

Decker's eyes narrowed at this. "A beautiful woman like you," he scoffed, "I find that hard to believe."

"Really?" Kate asked irritably. Not waiting for an answer, she explained, "I started dating one of my college professors almost right out of high school. He was a lot older than I was, but oh, he was quite the charmer. He strung me along for about six years until I found out he was cheating on me with just about every other intern that had come along. After that,

I pretty much focused on getting my doctorate and then after that, just my work."

Decker whistled. "Wow, that is rough." Then he grinned mischievously. "Well, if you're interested, Nikko's single, I think he might even be a little sweet on you. If you'd like, I can talk to him for you. I bet you two would really hit it off."

Kate beaned him with a nearby pillow.

"Hey, what's that for?" he asked, smiling, knowingly perfectly well the answer.

She got up and backpedaled until she reached the doorway. She lingered and they gazed at one another for a long moment. A heavy gust of wind assaulted the station and the room's only window pane rattled as the wind howled fiercely outside, bringing them back to their present dire situation. She didn't relish the idea of sleeping alone. Not with that thing running around outside. Rubbing her shoulders for warmth she found him still staring at her. She waited a heartbeat for him to say something, anything, and when he didn't she said, "I ... I should probably go."

Decker seemed like he was about to say something and she found herself wishing she had waited a second more.

She noticed he absentmindedly passed his hand over the scars on his chest, and after realizing his motion, and his audience, he seemed embarrassed by them. He could only nod back at her, seemingly in understanding, and then with a sad expression he said, "Sorry," and hurriedly found and slipped into a tight-fitting T-shirt. "And, uh, thanks for the water."

Kate nodded and it wasn't until she stepped out the doorway and eased the door shut that she realized what had happened. Decker had mistaken her shock over his multiple scars for disgust, which couldn't be farther from the truth. She wanted to open the door again and explain, but she had no idea of where to even begin.

This has got to be the worst first day of work, ever.

Even though her own quarters were only across the narrow hall, she sure as heck wasn't crazy about sleeping in her room alone with Bear-asaurus Rex outside on the loose. She fought the urge to grab her mattress off the bed and toss it inside Decker's quarters, on the floor, beside his bed. Hardly appropriate. And she wasn't sure what kind of message that would send.

Instead she entered inside the more modest quarters, slipped out of her boots and lay down on the bed. For a time, she just lay there staring at the ceiling and shivering, and not just from the freezing cold.

Eugene, Sierra, Sanjay, and Bill were all dead. She didn't know why, but the realization was only just hitting her now. Without meaning to, or wanting to, silent tears fell upon her pillow.

And she hated herself for it.

Chapter 15

Day Two

The next morning, by the time Kate came downstairs from the third floor, she felt refreshed. Exhausted from her previous day, she had slept like a log last night. And it was amazing how a long hot shower could lift your spirit.

Always darkest before the dawn.

She was having a hard time interpreting her feelings for Decker. Her life had never been more chaotic, and surrounded by so much death and fear, now seemed hardly the time for a romance, as if an action man like Detective James Decker would ever be permanently interested in a bookworm like her.

"Good morning, Sleeping Beauty," Vickers said, sitting at the kitchen counter and smiling knowingly.

Kate grinned. "And good morning to you too, Detective Vickers." Kate glanced around and saw none of the men were around.

Seeing this, Vickers explained, "Decker's downstairs with Sgt. Jenkins, Grimm and Nikko are still upstairs sleeping."

"What about the storm?"

"Still raging."

Sgt. Jenkins must have whipped up another one of his delicious country breakfasts because the kitchen air was still permeated with the smell of bacon and eggs. "Oh, I'm starving. Please tell me there's some of the Sergeant's cooking left?"

"Try the fridge," Vickers said, still grinning like a cat.

Kate found some leftovers and heated them up in the microwave. While she waited for her breakfast to warm, Vickers asked with mock innocence. "Sleep well?"

"Detective Vickers, I suspect you know very well that I did, despite your little attempts to find me a bunk mate," she answered, practically giggling. *Geez, we're worse than two school girls.*

Vickers nodded, laughing with her. After a moment of comfortable silence, Kate felt as though she could take the risk. "Vickers, can I ask you something?"

The behavioral signals expert read her like a book and said, "You want to know how his wife died." When Kate nodded, Vickers took a long sip from her bottled water before answering. "Like most Troopers in Alaska, Decker was a pilot; and in his case, he even owned his own bush plane."

Kate found that hard to believe when she remembered how frightened Decker had appeared on the flight coming up, but said nothing.

"About five years ago, he and his family flew into the interior to the little town of Bettles to visit Julie's parents. Do you know where that is?" When Kate shook her head, Vick explained, "Well, all you need to know is that it's real remote. Anyway, they were visiting his wife's parents out in the bush when their youngest boy started to arrive a month early. There had been complications with Julie's first pregnancy so Dex knew he had to get them both to the nearest hospital, about a hundred miles away. He left little Alex with her grandparents and they flew for the nearest hospital in Fairbanks. A freak storm appeared out of nowhere, and his plane was forced down. They crash landed just north of Fairbanks. Even though Dex had broken both legs in the crash and was seriously wounded, he managed to deliver their baby boy, but Julie had lost too much blood. Dex once told me that Julie laid eyes on her baby, smiled, and then was gone." Vickers paused for a moment, and took another long sip of water. "When the rescuers finally arrived, they found the baby wrapped up in a warm blanket sleeping comfortably on Dex's chest. He spent nearly a year recovering in the hospital after that. Even though a board of inquiry with the FAA cleared him of any wrongdoing, he still blames himself for Julie's death. He's hated flying ever since."

"Oh, that's awful."

Kate suddenly recalled the very first time she had laid eyes on Decker. No wonder he'd been so terrified. She felt bad for thinking it comical. She remembered the two smiling children in the photograph and asked, "How are his kids holding up?"

"They have their days; they're raised mostly by Julie's parents. Dex plans on taking early retirement next spring so he can reconnect with them."

As much as Kate wanted to learn more about Decker, she started remembering what she had found out about the dig site, and whether or not to tell the detectives about her findings. Finally she asked, "Are we any closer to finding out who did this?"

"No, but I think we all know what happened to your friends!" came a loud voice.

It was Nikko.

As he walked into the kitchen what was immediately apparent was that his native accent had thickened and his speech was as loud as it was slurred.

Had he been drinking?

"Oh yeah, Nikko? How's that?" Vickers asked, annoyance in her voice. Obviously she also had noticed his slurred speech. When Nikko turned away to rummage through his gear bag, Vick tipped her hand up to her mouth like she was drinking.

Nikko found what he was searching for and started to pull out a silver coffee thermos, but then slowly realizing he had company chose to put it back in his bag. "In my village, they would talk about the Tunqqun-qatiq." When he saw them both staring at him with puzzled looks on their faces, he explained, "It's Inupiaq slang in my village for White Death."

Vickers poured him a cup of steaming hot coffee and handed it to him. When Nikko took a sip, Kate could see his hand was trembling.

His eyes vacant, Nikko said, "I thought it was only a legend, or they were just talking about this really big polar bear, or maybe it was just another stupid parable about respecting the environment that my grandfather was always going on about. He even claimed to have seen it once. I never believed him. Thought it was the booze talking. In the end that's what got him, ya know ... the booze. As I was saying, as a young man he was hunting for seal way out on the forbidden ice, bout twenty, no, thirty miles north of here. Anyways, he comes across a dead polar bear. But the funny thing was, the bear was lying in pieces, like something had ripped it limb from limb. About then my grandfather hears this horrendous howl." Nikko reared back his head and let out a deep, guttural howling noise that was as loud as it was ominous. "Anyway, he takes cover behind a snow berm and he sees it. He said it was one-and-a-half times bigger than the biggest polar bear he'd ever seen in his life. And my grandfather has hunted a lot of polar bears. Anyway, I remember whenever he would tell the story, he would always say that the bear looked kind of funny, like nothing he had ever seen before." He turned towards Vickers for a moment. "You know?" He stared at her for a long time, and then said. "You're a pretty lady."

"Thanks, Nikko," Vickers replied, smiling, and pitying the young man at the same time.

"What happened to your grandfather?" Kate asked.

"What?" Nikko asked.

"Your grandfather, with that thing out on the ice."

"Oh yeah, that ..." he said quietly, then raised his voice. "He got the hell out of there. He said he ain't never run so fast in his life. He knew his only chance was to leave the forbidden ice, and never return." When he gazed up from his fingers and stared slowly at the two of them, it seemed to Kate that the youth had gone out of him instantly. "All I know is, none of us are ever gonna leave this place. Not alive anyway. No, sir." Then studied his audience once more, he giggled and said, "I mean ... no, Ma'am." He chuckled again at his own joke.

"How about we watch the video recording and judge for ourselves?"

This time the voice belonged to Detective Decker. He was followed closely by Sgt. Jenkins.

"What did you find?" Vickers asked immediately.

After last night, Kate wasn't sure how to behave. Should she call him James or Detective Decker? Were they friends now, or was that just a good cop comforting one of many victims?

Decker didn't give her much time to think more about it. Clearly he had found something new, his tone all business. "While we were testing the radios downstairs, I noticed a little red light near the ceiling."

"We found surveillance equipment," Sgt. Jenkins jumped in proudly. "Hidden pretty good, too."

"Yeah, the Sergeant had to rip the wiring right out of the wall, but we finally tracked it back to a digital recording device hidden in one of the cabinets downstairs."

Kate froze for a second and wondered if they had found the safe, too. She realized that she still hadn't told Decker or anyone else about the dig site. *Will they arrest me for withholding evidence?*

"I don't remember seeing any cameras." Kate said, desperately trying to keep the nervousness out of her voice.

Did Vicker's eyebrow just go up?

If Decker was aware of her nervousness, he didn't show it. Instead he nodded toward the ceiling. "See that little red dot up there? That's a surveillance camera. They're all over the facility."

"Now we can see what really attacked those scientists," Sgt. Jenkins offered.

"Or we can see who's been staging these elaborate hoaxes," Decker countered.

Vickers teased, "So Dex, I guess when a big ol' prehistoric bear bites you on the butt, you'll have a logical explanation for that, too."

"Let's just watch the playback and find out," Decker said wryly.

—— <> ——

A short while later, everyone had gathered in the recreation room. They crowded around the plasma screen like six kids about to watch a good horror movie.

"I wish I had some popcorn."

"Shut up, Grimm," Vickers said instantly.

Kate made a mental note to ask Vickers why she hated Dr. Grimm so much. Sure the guy was annoying, and certainly weird, but she sensed there was something more to Vickers's animosity.

Decker had decided that seeing how everyone's life was in jeopardy, they all had a right to see what was on the tape. When they had first hooked up the DVR to the big screen, the view jumped annoyingly back and forth between all the hidden cameras. But with a few swift key strokes, Grimm had set it to play back only the footage gathered by the camera on the second floor. It was weird seeing the dead researchers come back to life and go out of the room that they now occupied. It was almost as though they were watching their ghosts.

"Fast forward," Decker ordered.

After a time, Grimm slowed the recording down again and Kate saw footage of Sierra, Banks, the engineer Bill Peterson, and the two assistants, Sanjay and Charlotte, all eating at the table together.

"No, keep going. This is two days ago," Vick announced, noting the time stamp.

Grimm fast forwarded the image up until the wall suddenly exploded. He paused right on the cause.

Vickers yelled, "Stop right there!"

Sgt. Jenkins exclaimed, "Holy Crap!"

Decker was silent, and Grimm appeared as though he was about to cry.

Everyone in the room now knew beyond a shadow of a doubt the reason for the scientists' demise.

Kate's understanding of the real world collapsed in on itself, and Vickers breathed aloud, "Oh my God. Nikko's right. None of us are getting out of here alive."

Two Days Ago

Chapter 16

Eugene Banks

A thin crescent moon hung over the distant horizon. In sharp contrast to the twilight sky and perpetual snow, the silhouettes of the Brooks Range mountains sixty miles to the south stood like glowing temples to the night sky.

To some, the view of the Arctic Circle's landscape was breathtaking, majestic, and perhaps even awe inspiring. To others, like geologist Dr. Eugene Banks ... it was a crap hole.

What a frozen wasteland of death.

Banks shivered from the cold despite his heavy-duty Arctic parka. He pulled his fur-lined hood tighter over his face. Out here on the island, the temperature hovered around twenty below. The air was so thin that breathing was difficult, even labored. *A veritable paradise,* he thought, following the luminescent guide wires, as he trudged across the slushy ice, back towards the research facility. The wind howled upon his back like a starving beast. Even after six months, he still felt the urge to stop in his tracks, turn around and check for a stalking predator, but it was always the same, nothing but the vicious ... relentless ... Arctic wind.

He never would have agreed to work in this frozen hellhole, but Sierra Banks, the love of his life since elementary school, had chosen this fate for him. *How many years had he followed her all over Alaska? Ten, twenty?*

Oh, how he hated this dreary state. He'd only moved to Alaska because he wanted to be close to his lovely Athabascan wife. He knew if he had declined to go into fieldwork with her, she would have just taken off without him. Although he never asked, mainly because he knew the answer, it was pretty clear which was more important to Sierra between her career or their marriage. So, once again, he packed his thermal long-johns into his bags and they were off once more.

Banks was sick and tired of all his colleagues back at Cambridge telling him how lucky he was to be drowning on this ice-cold inhospitable island, so obviously unwelcome to mankind.

He trudged up the trail, which was made easier by the snowmobiles that shuttled back and forth, watching the research station come into view. Tilting his head back, he could see the massive Spam Can, its outer shell glowing softly from the reflected moonlight.

Once the ruins had been found on the island, the prefabricated facility had been brought in by barge in three stages and then reassembled. Even Banks had to admire the engineering of the state-of-the-art research station.

Ruins, hah. That's a laugh. Sure, the jade totem was a significant find, but Banks was hardly impressed with the overgrown fragments of stone that suggested pictographs.

He shivered, a fresh gust of wind pelting him as he opened the outer bear cage. Careful to close the door behind him first, he then opened the outer hatch. When he finally moved inside the arctic entry and saw everyone else's parkas on their racks, he realized that once again he was last to arrive for chow. They were all probably upstairs eating while here he was still shuttling artifacts across the ice. *Isn't that what the interns are supposed to be for?*

Removing his hat, Banks looked at his reflection, a man with an oval face, bright green eyes beneath round-framed glasses. He felt he was still a good-looking man at the age of fifty-two, even if he did have a slight pot belly and often wore a cap to hide his heavily receding hairline.

When he arrived on the second floor, everyone had gathered in the recreation room. Or at least almost everyone. Scanning around the rec room, Banks did not see his wife.

Bill Peterson, an older heavyset gentleman who fancied himself an engineer but in reality was nothing more than a glorified handyman whose only job was to keep the lights on and the toilets flushing, greeted him first. At the moment, he was lounging in his big easy chair by the window while the interns, Charlotte and Sanjay, were nearby shooting a game of pool.

Nice, I seem to be the only one working around here.

"Hey, Banks, bout time you came in out of the cold," Bill said. Bill was also a short timer, and over the last two weeks he had delighted in telling anyone who would listen about all the things he was going to do once he got back home to Texas, most of which involved eating at his favorite restaurants. It was maddening listening to him. *Didn't he realize that there were other people who missed civilization too? People who weren't scheduled to leave until next summer? It might as well be an eternity.*

"Hey, what ya got there?"

"What?" Banks asked, then gazed down and realized he was still holding the strange sea shell he had found at the dig site. "I'm not sure. I think it may be some sort of pre-Neolithic pictograph fragmentation."

"Really? That's great, where'd you find it?" Bill asked him enthusiastically.

Weally, dat's great, where'd you find it, Banks repeated in his head, automatically adding a whine disdainfully. Instead he answered aloud, "I found it in the new chamber just behind the totem."

But Bill Peterson didn't hear him. His beady, unintelligent eyes were already studying the strange relic. Eventually, Bill frowned and said "Looks more like an oversized flute to me."

"No, Bill," Banks stated irritably. "I don't think so. If you saw the rest of the dig site, then you would know that." He noticed the intern, Charlotte, seemed to take notice of his abruptness, but she said nothing.

But just as he should have suspected, the big stupid oaf didn't even realize that he was being insulted. Unfazed, Bill lifted his meaty palms skyward and said, "Hey, whatever you say, pal, but my kid played the clarinet for years, and I know a flute when I see one."

Banks could not believe he had bantered with this moron for this long. Even back in Anchorage, when he was a professor at the university, he had never had to suffer the indignities of someone like Bill Peterson.

Without warning, Bill scooped up the valuable artifact and before Banks could stop him, he said, "See, there's even a mouthpiece right here," and blew into it.

"Mr. Peterson, if you would kindly give that back," Banks started to say, but the most unearthly musical notes came out of the fragment.

Bill was grinning like a circus clown. "See? I told you, it's a flute."

Charlotte the intern came over and said, "Do it again, Bill."

As Bill blew into the mouthpiece a second time, he began experimenting by covering different holes with different fingers. The result was as expected.

"That's amazing," Banks stammered, and he meant it. *How did I not know it was a flute? How did I miss that? I mean, I thought it was just a carving or something.* They were hearing notes generated by a musical instrument that had not been played in over ten thousand years. And it was all thanks to this, well ... oafish janitor.

Bill stopped his playing and turned the relic over in his hands. "Hey, check this out," he said pointing to a small circular hole on the end opposite the mouthpiece. I bet you can put some string through this eyehole."

"Like a necklace," Charlotte offered.

"Hold this," he said handing the flute to Charlotte. He then took a piece of black leather out of his oversized tool belt. "Yeah, this is perfect," he muttered to himself, then strung the leather string through the eyehole.

Banks heard himself say, "I really don't think that's such a good idea, Bill, this a very valuable artifact."

But Bill finished threading the eyehole and tied the open ends to one another. "There," he stated proudly. "Now you can wear it around your neck, just like I bet those ancient folks did that you're always yammering on about." Without warning, Bill stepped forward and draped the flute on its leather string around Banks's neck.

Banks gently fingered the flute necklace resting on his chest. He hated to admit it, but he was impressed. "Uh, thanks, Bill," was all he could manage.

"Think of it as a going away gift. I'm shipping out tomorrow, ya know."

Instead of beating Bill the handyman over the head with his new flute, Banks asked, "Have you seen Sierra?"

Bill hiked his fleshy opposable thumb (which was probably the only thing that separated him from his ape cousins) back to one of three doors exiting the central hub area. "I think she's still in the lab. You know Sierra, she'd starve if we didn't slide a dish of food underneath her door," Peterson said, smiling that maddening grin of his.

"Hh-mm, uh-huh, okay then," Banks said, eager to conclude any more of this mindless repartee. "I'm just going to go and see how she's doing."

"All right then, partner. I'll be sure and swing by your quarters and see you before I take off tomorrow morning."

"You be sure and do that, Bill," Banks said, and then turned to head down the hallway.

That was when Charlotte screamed.

Banks spun back towards the rec room and exclaimed, "Oh my God in heaven."

"What, whatsa matter with you two?" Bill asked, moving over to Charlotte as quickly as a man his girth was capable of.

But Banks couldn't speak. He could only point.

The big oaf finally turned his head towards the window. Standing outside, on its hind legs, was a polar bear staring inside. Even though they were on the second floor, the enormous bear's head was able to just barely peek over the bottom of the window frame.

"What? Him?" Bill asked. "He's harmless, just curious is all. He can't hurt you while you're in here."

Banks stammered, "But I was just out *there*. He could have eaten me."

"Nah ... Here, watch this." Bill rolled up a newspaper and whapped it on the window. The bear blinked twice at him. "Go on now, shoo." Bill whapped the window a third time and the bear dropped down out of view. "See? Like I told ya. Harmless."

Visibly shaken, Banks could only nod his head. That was it. Dig site or not, he wasn't sticking around for another minute, not a single one. He was really going to put his foot down this time. Sierra was either coming with him, or he was flying back to Anchorage all by his lonesome.

Banks turned on his heel and left the common area in search of his wife.

Bill called down the hallway after him, "Hey, don't forget, I'm waking your butt up early tomorrow morning to say good-bye."

"You be sure and do that, Bill," Banks said, and then he went back downstairs towards the lab. Damn, how he wished that guy would just drop dead.

Yeah. That'd be great.

Chapter 17

Sierra Banks

When Dr. Eugene Banks entered the lab, he found his wife Sierra exactly where he had left her this morning, standing over her latest find that was lying on one of the lab's examination tables. Her latest specimen, a granite statue, lay in pieces, several broken appendages around one fully intact torso, resembling an unsolved puzzle.

If the empty coffee cups and uneaten food stacked on the tables around her were any indication, she had probably been rooted to the same spot since his departure. He wasn't sure which attracted him to her more: her unbelievable work ethic, her pure unadulterated scientific genius, or her youthful, muscular body covered in perfect olive-tanned skin.

He purposely kept the flute out of her line of sight by keeping it concealed beneath the folds of his jacket, so as to bring it up at just the right time. Maybe he'd even do a little ventriloquism for added effect.

Oh, how droll.

Instead he asked, "How's the autopsy coming?" He knew she was still furious with him about the fight they had had last night. He had brought up one too many times the fact that it was her fault that he was here in this miserable, foreboding hellhole.

"Same," she answered curtly. But he knew the curtness was not so much out of her irritation with him but the way she always spoke when she was focused on her work.

He knew Sierra didn't like the broken statue on the table before her, not at all. She had said as much, and he knew it gave her the creeps as it managed to manifest itself in her nightmares for the past several nights.

Whether it was of a real creature or a mythological deity, the stone carving was ominous. Jagged teeth, enormous claws, and a thick muscled body matted in fur.

Even motionless, the sculpture gave him the same feeling he got when he had seen a great white shark strung up once on a pier off the coast of Florida, waiting any moment for it to spring to life and snatch him up in its jaws. Yet, at the same time, Sierra was enthralled by it.

This wasn't the only image of the demon, either. Before finding the statue in the ruins, they had discovered a pictograph of it, depicting the demon at the end of its master's chains, graphically destroying stick figure enemies before it.

So far they hadn't found much else since the totem chamber. It was as though the people who had built it had all suddenly vanished, like the Aztecs or citizens of Pompeii. One minute they were going about their daily lives—cooking, writing, dealing—and the next, they all simply vanished.

Sierra was convinced that there had to be some kind of explanation. They just hadn't found it yet. Fortunately, in a few more months, it wouldn't be his problem anymore. Their employers had promised new replacements that would rotate in and then they could finally leave this miserable ice box once and for all.

Banks picked up one of the more jagged pieces of the statue and turned it in his hand. He was always surprised how heavy even the smallest of fragments were. "Have you picked out a name for him yet?" he asked, still waiting to spring his surprise musical instrument.

At the question, his wife gazed up at him. "What makes you think it's a him?"

Examining the piece more closely in his hand, he offered, again trying to be humorous, "Well for one thing, whatever it was, it had hair all over its body."

"We're not naming it, at least not until we learn out more about it," she said. She was obviously frustrated that another day's work had revealed no new findings, or the reason why everyone had so swiftly vanished. "Now give me that before you break it," she said, reaching for the fragment in his hands.

"Be careful. 'He' could be dangerous," he said teasingly as she yanked the artifact away from him.

"Ouch!" she exclaimed, then quickly replaced the fragment on the table. Before he could stop her, she practically ripped off her plastic glove and reflexively put her sliced finger in her mouth to stop the bleeding.

"See, dangerous," he said lightheartedly and then, worried that the cut was worse than he'd thought, he asked with genuine concern in his voice, "You okay?"

"Yeah," she said, removing her finger from her mouth, the tiny cut in her skin having already clotted. "I just nicked myself."

"Well, just to be safe, wash your hands really well, and in the future, could you please not put your hands in your mouth after touching centuries-old artifacts."

She rolled her eyes, but he could see that she felt stupid for having made such an obvious mistake.

Now is the time.

"Well, I was going to save this for later but seeing how you could use a pick me up ..." He pulled the flute out of his shirt and held it up for Sierra to see. Her eyes went wide with wonder, and she quickly donned a fresh glove, eagerly getting ready to take it from him.

He held up his hand to stop her, and before she could ask, he said, "I found it in the chamber behind the jade totem."

Sierra couldn't even speak; she just continued to stare at the flute, whose carvings seemed almost alive, even after the passage of thousands of years, surviving a span of time that began long before the Ancient Pyramids rose in Egypt.

"That's not all. Listen to this," he said, then blew on the flute. The air filled with musical notes unheard for ten millennia.

Sierra's eyes went wide.

She stepped forward and fingered the flute still dangling by the piece of leather tied around his neck. "This is unprecedented."

As she marveled over this latest find, Banks inhaled the sweet scent of her hair. Even after all these years of being together, he was always amazed at just how beautiful she was. Even now, it was so cute the way she studied the relic, so much so he wanted to lean forward and just kiss her. But more pressing matters needed to be addressed. And he knew it was now or never. He took a deep breath and braced himself for the task that lay ahead. It didn't take a psychic to know the fight that would ensue. Despite this, he asked her anyway. "Maybe it's time we contact some of our colleagues about our findings? Kate Foster, for example."

"Euuuu-geeeene," she said, stretching out his name to show her frustration with him. He had learned that in their last fifteen years of marriage, the longer she stretched it out, the more irritated she was with him. It had been his secret Sierra-barometer that he lived by. "We've been through this already. Once we go public, this place will be crawling with scientists fighting over the dig site. Who knows how much damage could be done. Our employers know what they are doing. Besides, do you really think the world is ready to learn that an ancient civilization existed, predating the Sumerians by ten thousand years?"

Since the time he and Sierra had met as kids, dating all through high school and college, Banks had taken a lot of garbage from his buddies for always giving in to his wife's desires. But it wasn't that he was a pushover, as everyone around him suspected. He certainly wouldn't have gotten the "assignment of the millennia" if he had been just some whipped husband. The truth was, he just loved her. Loved her with every fiber of his being. He had ever since he had first laid eyes on her that fateful day by the lake back in Oregon, at his best friend's house where they had all grown up together. And if keeping the dig site a secret for a little longer was what would make Sierra happy, then that was what she was going to get. Besides, he not only admired her passion for her chosen line of work, he admired her passion for wanting to share it with the rest of humanity. She was the best of them both. Without her, he knew he was nothing more than a cantankerous old fool. He decided the world could wait a little while longer.

"Fine," he said, beaten. "Let me just grab a shower and maybe we can both eat some dinner." And with that said, he exited the lab and headed for the personnel quarters up on the third floor.

—— < > ——

Sierra watched her husband go. She knew she should have stopped him. She could have at least thanked him for finding the flute. She knew that without him, she would have certainly burnt out long ago. Everyone like her needed a Eugene in their life to ground them. Without their steady, enduring love to keep her feet on the ground, she knew she would have just spiraled off into the cosmos, lost in the joy of scientific discovery.

Sierra loved her husband, and she also knew he was right. Just as soon as they made enough copies of everything they had recorded so far and hid the copies for safekeeping, she'd tell him to make the call. She tried to imagine Kate's reaction when they first shared their findings with her, especially the jade totem. The poor girl. Even now, she was being raked over the coals for everything they had confirmed to be true. Well, it wouldn't be much longer before Kate could see for herself.

It took her about another half-hour to replace the relics she had been studying in their respective trays for safekeeping. Satisfied they would be safe until morning, she removed her gloves once more and began washing up in the nearby sink.

Tonight before bed, she would tell her husband just how much she loved him and appreciated all he had done. How after their rotation was up they would finally settle down and she would give him what he wanted most, a family. Sure, they weren't spring chickens anymore, but it wasn't unheard of to have kids at middle-age.

Sierra smiled at the thought of making her husband so happy.

Just as she reached for a towel to dry her hands, the horrific screaming began.

Chapter 18

Bill Peterson

After visiting the kitchen and devouring another Bumstead sandwich, Bill Peterson dropped back down into his easy chair like a guided missile made of sandbags and resumed reading his magazine by the rec room window.

He had just started reading an article on the diminishing Everglades when he noticed a large shadow rising up over his magazine. Had he turned his head, Bill might have realized this shadow's owner was much larger than its earlier predecessor. Instead, Bill rolled up his periodical, and without so much as glancing over his shoulder, wrapped it on the window behind him.

"No! Bad bear!"

The creature's head slowly dropped down, and its shadow diminished.

Satisfied, Bill once more returned to his article about the Florida Everglades, and he began fantasizing about visiting someplace equally warm and tropical.

The window behind him didn't so much shatter as the entire wall exploded inward. Even in the chaos, it was immediately apparent that the monstrosity that leapt through the wall was far larger, and greyer in color, than any polar bear.

Before Bill Peterson could even cry out in alarm, the giant bear dove on him, pile-driving him into the floor. It immediately latched onto Bill's head, painting the floor with his crimson blood. Bill started screaming, a shrill and terrible shrieking noise, over and over again.

The two interns playing pool instantly dropped their pool cues and ran down the hallway, Sanjay running for the unauthorized rifle he had hidden in his quarters, Charlotte frantically chasing after him.

Sanjay was almost to the stairwell when he was struck heavily from behind by Charlotte's flailing body. The creature had raked Charlotte's back with one claw and her back split into two pieces, her body exploding in a spray of blood.

Unlike Bill, Charlotte hadn't even had time for a proper scream.

Sanjay fell violently into the entrance to the stairwell. He risked a quick glimpse back at Charlotte and saw the monster furiously smashing her body again and again into the walls and ceiling. The creature's enormous girth filled the entire hallway, and Sanjay could hear the walls crumple beneath its attack.

Rifle forgotten, Sanjay flung himself down the stairs in an act of desperation.

—— <> ——

In the bathroom on the third floor, Eugene Banks had just finished his shower and was pulling on his shirt when he first heard the loud series of explosions emanating from downstairs. He nearly jumped out of his skin when he heard the screaming, a shrill and terrible shrieking noise, repeated over and over again.

What the hell is going on down there? Is this some kind of sick joke?

Leaving his shirt unbuttoned, Banks flew down the stairs as fast as his bare feet could carry him, torn between anger and fear. This had to be another one of Bill Peterson's childish practical jokes! Well, Banks had had enough. He was going to call the university and demand Bill's immediate termination.

He reached the second floor and hesitated for a second, fear overtaking the anger. It was a joke, right? But people didn't shriek like that for merely a prank. And what was that loud crashing sound? It sounded like an explosion.

Moving more cautiously now, he opened the door and took a step inside the rec hall.

The first thing he noticed was that the emergency lighting had kicked on and everything was bathed in a supernatural crimson color. All other overhead lighting had been smashed beyond repair. Only a few flickering bulbs remained. One lighting fixture was swinging from ripped out wires, sparking electrical juice, leaving most of the room bathed in shifting shadows.

Sierra was nowhere to be seen. No one was. What little he could see of the hallway was crumpled walls, seeming to confirm his theory that something indeed had exploded. But if that was the case, where was the smell, burn marks, or smoke?

He took one small step forward. Other than the sparking of the light fixture, and the crunching underfoot of the glittering debris of shattered glass, the only sound was his own labored breath.

He entered the hallway, anger and fear becoming shock, oblivious to the broken shards of glass cutting his bare feet.

"Sierra?" he said, his voice cracking, his heart pounding in his chest. Nothing he had ever read about described the level of fear he was feeling now.

Too many shadows. I need a flashlight.

He tried to recall where the nearest one might be. All he could come up with was that the storage locker on the first floor had an emergency flashlight mounted next to it, which would certainly do him no good up here.

He had taken a few more careful steps down the darkened corridor when he felt a heavy droplet of water stream down his forehead and the side of his face. He wiped it away, but did a double-take when his peripheral vision noticed it wasn't water on the back of his hand. It was blood.

He wiped the blood from his hand and found no cut on his hand or on the side of his face. He then probed his scalp with his fingers but did not find any sort of wound.

Then where did the blood come from?

He felt another droplet of liquid strike the back of his hand as he was checking his scalp again.

Not wanting to, he lifted his eyes upwards. What he saw there was something that caused his stomach to churn repeatedly. It was as though someone had mopped the ceiling with a bucket of blood.

Resisting the powerful urge to vomit, he saw a bloody pile of human tissue slammed onto the ceiling, as though someone had squashed it there beneath a giant foot. He could just barely make out a ruined, distorted face, frozen in agony.

Oh my ... is that ... Charlotte?

A trail of blood started at the pulpy mess that was left of Charlotte, then went across the ceiling and continued down the hallway to the rec room.

The smell hit him like a hammer and he emptied the entire contents of his stomach in a single heave. He had to hold on to the wall for support, and just when he thought he might pass out from lack of air, it was over. He sucked in a gulp full of air.

Have to move, have to find Sierra.

He leaned forward and found himself moving down the corridor, following the trail of blood overhead as though walking through some nightmare.

The blood trail on the ceiling that had started near the stairwell abruptly ended in the recreation room. It seemed as though the gruesome paint brush had finally run out of paint.

"Sierra?" he asked in a rasping, frightened voice. "Bill?" What he wouldn't give to hear that big oaf's loud boisterous voice now.

At first, he didn't see anyone, only the overturned furniture and the wrecked lighting system.

Then he saw what was left of Bill Peterson. His remains were sticking out from behind an overturned table. Both legs were missing.

For some reason, Bill's body was what convinced him that all of this was real. Some small part of his mind had still been hoping this was all some elaborate ruse. A trick. The loud noise, the screams, and even the bloody mess on the ceiling, could all be faked. But now, seeing Bill's still form, with his legs serrated like that ... this ... this was definitely real.

A gust of wind blew inside the gaping hole in the wall, the icy blast shocking him into some semblance of wakefulness. *Funny how he hadn't noticed the wall was missing until now.*

Banks recalled the polar bear outside the window and was immediately certain of the culprit. This wasn't any explosion.

A well of anger grew up inside him. He turned towards Bill's crumpled form and screamed, "Totally harmless, huh? Well, do you believe me now?"

It was hard to stay angry at a guy who was missing his legs, arm, and face … and life …

Suddenly, he heard more screaming. This time from the first floor.

Oh no! … Sierra.

Banks fought every fiber in his being that was telling him to run, go back upstairs, and lock himself back in the bathroom. After all, he was no hunter; he'd never even shot a gun in his life. Even if he had, where would he find one? The thought of escaping in one of the tractors sprang to mind. He knew that anything was better than going downstairs towards that infernal wailing, fearing what he would inevitably find.

But that's exactly what a loving husband does, he faces his fears for the one he loves most. And that was exactly what he was going to do or die trying.

It sucks being a coward.

Summoning what little courage he possessed, he turned back the way he had come. Earlier he had rushed down to the rec room not knowing anything, not knowing what he would find. But this next threshold, the one that led down to the first floor, the one that led towards the screaming and not away from it, needed a whole new, different level of courage. Courage he didn't possess. For he knew things now. Bad things. This wasn't some cheap, cliché horror movie he was watching on Friday night with the interns. He was living it.

He knew about the blood trail splattered on the ceiling. He had seen what was left of poor Bill Peterson. He knew that whatever had killed Bill and Charlotte was most likely still roaming around downstairs.

But Sierra …

He entered the stairwell and walked downstairs in a dazed state. Eventually, he found himself standing before the doorway that would reveal the horrors that awaited him on the first floor. He felt his heart pounding so hard he thought his heart might explode out of his chest. He knew he couldn't delay any longer. He had to go in there. He had to find out what had happened to his wife.

Open it, you coward. Your wife might be still alive and you're just standing here in the stairwell, quivering like a frightened little girl.

When the screaming began again, he shuddered as much as if he had been shot by a bullet. More so when the screaming stopped as abruptly as it had begun.

Silence.

He wasn't sure which was worse, the screaming or the silence. But he knew he couldn't stay in the stairwell forever.

Holding his breath, his hand found the door and he eased it inward. Not much, only a narrow crack.

Do it for Sierra, do it for Sierra ... do it for her.

Shaking uncontrollably from sheer terror, he slowly opened the door the rest of the way.

And Professor Eugene Banks finally crossed his last threshold.

Chapter 19

Sanjay

Sierra practically flew out of her lab and into the main laboratory on the first floor.

A second later, Sanjay vaulted out of the stairwell with his arms flailing like a puppet jacked up on cocaine. "We have to leave!" he shouted at her. "And we have to do it right now!" He grabbed her roughly by the wrist and dragged her towards the exit.

"What happened up there? We can't leave. What about Bill and Charlotte, what about my husband?"

"I said, run!"

When they reached the exit, Sanjay shoved a heavy coat into her arms and quickly climbed into one of his own. His face was one of pure terror and he was yelling every word. "They're gone! Okay? And we will be too if we don't leave right *now*!"

"Sanjay, stop it, you're scaring me."

Sanjay didn't hear her. Even before she could put her jacket on he dragged her over to the inner hatch, spun the wheel, and stepped inside. When she didn't follow him into the arctic entry, he screamed at her, "C'mon!" When she shook her head, he reached over and pulled her roughly through the hatch and slammed the door.

Sierra felt tears streaming down her face and heard herself sobbing as Sanjay spun the wheel to the outer hatch. "There's no time, there's no time! We have to go!" he kept repeating, as though it were his new mantra. He opened the outer hatch and stepped outside into the bear cage. The frigid air blew into the entryway, reminding her that she still held the big coat in her arms and was not wearing it on her body.

Seeing that she still wasn't following, Sanjay turned back towards her. "Sierra, you have to come with me, now. Come on!"

She shook her head briskly. "I'm not leaving, not without my husband."

Sanjay took only a moment to let this sink in. "I'm sorry." He turned back towards the exit and was about to open the door to the bear cage when he saw the monstrosity standing outside the bars.

The massive creature rose up on its hind legs, towering over the cage. After studying Sanjay for only a moment, it slammed both paws down on the cage.

Sanjay tripped over his own feet and fell backwards. He hit his head on the lip of the hatch, but didn't lose consciousness. Shaken, he pressed his back against the outer wall.

Like a rabid dog, the prehistoric monster was furiously snapping at him through the bars of the cage. The thing slammed the cage again and again, damaging it severely, but unable to get at its prey.

Seeing this, Sanjay shakily rose to his feet and said in an unhinged voice, "Hah, hah-ha-hah. That's right, you bastard, you can't get in, can you?!"

Sierra's eyes were wide with horror, screamed, "Sanjay, get out of there!"

Sanjay turned towards her, some relief returning to his voice. "It's okay, he can't get us. He can't get through the ..."

CRASH!

Sanjay screamed as he immediately fell and was violently dragged backwards towards the exit. Instinctively his hands reached up and clenched either side of the hatch.

Sierra dropped her jacket and grabbed Sanjay by his coat.

Sanjay began sobbing. "Not like this," then louder at the bear, "Not like this!"

There was a loud, bone-crunching sound. Sanjay screamed in pain and then was ripped from the doorway.

In seconds, Sanjay and the creature had vanished into the storm.

When her lungs refused to hold air any longer, Sierra heard the sound of her own breath as she exhaled heavily. Choking oxygen back into quivering lungs, she slowly regained her feet and backed away from the hatch. "Sanjay … Eugene?" She waited for a response. The howling wind was her only answer.

Then, she was grabbed from behind.

Chapter 20

Which One

It took several moments for Sierra to stop screaming.

She was shaking uncontrollably in his arms, but when she finally stopped fighting him and realized who had grabbed her she cried, "Eugene ... Oh, thank God. You're alive!"

Staring at the open arctic entry and ruined bear cage beyond, Banks didn't need to see Sanjay's body to know he was gone too.

"Sierra," he said soothingly, stroking her hair. "Sierra, I want you to get dressed."

She shook her head, "No, no, no. We can't go outside. Not with that ... thing running around."

He stroked her hair. "Sierra. We have to. This might be our only chance."

But then he glimpsed it out of the corner of his eye. A blackness, deeper than any shadow, rose up outside the bear cage. It was watching them.

The predator stepped out of the shadows of the storm and into the light of the arctic entry. It stood there, its eyes and nose feeding on their presence.

Now that the thing was in the light, he could see it had an unusually wide face and short broad muzzle, so that it resembled a lion rather than any of the North American bears that he was familiar with. As he studied its features, it charged. Its flesh rippled with motion as it ran.

Before he could utter a warning, the bear broke through the arctic entry and slammed into the two of them with the force of a runaway truck.

They both went flying.

The bear rose up on its hind legs as though trying to decide which of them it was going to devour first.

All he could manage was to prop himself up against a cabinet door, too stunned to speak or move. He glanced over at his wife. She struggled to her knees, but fell back to the floor, her body refusing to respond to her commands.

Detecting her movements, the bear dove on top of her first. It snatched her neck in its massive jaws and violently shook her to pieces.

When it finally dropped her torso to the floor, Eugene Banks could only stare at what was left of his wife's motionless form. But without his being aware of his own movements, he found himself turning to look at his wife's killer.

The grotesque visage of Sierra's remains was replaced with the bear standing over him and staring down at him with its mouth wide open. The leviathan's breath reeked of foul carrion. He wasn't even aware of the urine running down his leg.

He would have preferred it had surprised him, as it so obviously had Bill Peterson, Charlotte, and Sanjay. But instead, he alone was allowed the privilege of getting a good long look at it. *Aren't I the lucky one?* He doubted Bill Peterson had suffered anywhere near this long.

What are you waiting for?

The creature lowered its head and slid its jaws to either side of his trembling head.

Then stopped.

What the hell?

The bear's jaws faded from view and Banks heard its gigantic snout sniffing him. Then he realized, the bear wasn't sniffing him, but the flute around his neck.

With a puzzled expression, the bear turned its head to the side, as though curious why he hadn't said anything about it before. After a moment more of this, it sauntered back over to Sierra and slipped what was left of her body into its jaws.

Before exiting with its prey, it took one last look at him as if to say, "Is this okay?" then slipped back outside with Sierra still clutched in its maw.

Then the monstrous nightmare was gone.

Sanjay was gone, Charlotte was gone, the love of his life was gone, even that idiot Bill Peterson. They were all gone. There was no reason for him to go on.

But why me? Why did it spare ... me?

In the end, he supposed that it didn't matter.

As his vision blurred, he didn't fight the veil of darkness creeping up over his brain like a spider over an ensnared fly. He welcomed it.

He welcomed death.

Chapter 21

Seeing is Believing

Grimm pressed the stop button on the remote. They had seen it. And it was real.

Throughout the entire viewing, everyone had taken turns glancing at the boarded up hole to make sure it was still secure.

At one point, Decker had asked Kate if she wanted to excuse herself, but she had told him that she'd preferred to stay. Decker didn't appear happy about her decision, but he didn't make her leave either.

Sgt. Jenkins was the first one to rise from his chair. He appeared dazed. "I've got to try and warn the mainland."

"What?" Grimm asked, equally shocked, then, his voice escalating, "The mainland ... to hell with the mainland, what about us?"

Sgt. Jenkins marched over to the skinny scientist, and Kate thought he was going to hit him. Glaring down at Grimm still seated on the couch, Jenkins said, "There are over four thousand people working on the North Slope that need to be warned about that thing."

Grimm thought about it for a moment, then, his anger overcoming his cowardice, he spat, "Well, the last time I checked, the radio was still on the fritz, so you just go right ahead."

"Leroy," Detective Decker said under his breath. "Sergeant, you got this?"

Sergeant Jenkins just stood up straight, removed his ball cap and replaced it, and said. "I am going to try the radio again." And then he exited the room.

Grimm, practically in a delirium now, said "Maybe, maybe the bear was inserted digitally. I mean if they can make it look like a car can turn into a robot or invent a whole world of blue elves, they can do this, right?"

One glance from Decker and Vickers immediately shot down Grimm's movie-magic theory.

"What the hell was that thing?" Vickers breathed.

"Big, whatever it is," Decker mused.

"I-I told you," Grimm stuttered. "If we are to believe what we are seeing on the playback, that is the short-faced bear."

Vickers began rubbing her hands together almost furiously. "But what's it doing here? I thought you said they all died out ten thousand years ago."

"They did," Grimm answered, pushed a hand through his greasy bangs. "I mean, that's what scientists believe."

"We should go." This came from Nikko. Kate thought she could still detect an odor of alcohol coming from his labored breath. He had been quiet up until now. "Just load up in the tractors and go, man. The hell with the weather."

"Yeah," Grimm agreed readily. "Nikko's right. I'm with him. Let's get in the tractors and bug the hell outta here."

Decker answered. "Nobody's going anywhere. That storm is still in Phase III."

"Hey, screw the storm, all right?" Grimm pointed to the television set. "I'll take my chances with the storm any day of the week over getting crapped out on the ice by that thing."

Decker rose to his full height. Very calmly he said, "It would be suicide to leave in the storm, and you know it." When it appeared as though Grimm and Nikko were about to protest further, he raised his voice only a little. "You wouldn't get far in the tractors. And you would be more exposed to that ..." Decker struggled for a word to describe the monstrosity they had just seen. "... thing out there, a lot more than you would be in here." When he glanced at her, he could see in her eyes just how frightened she really was.

He added, "Don't worry Kate. The Sergeant and I can fortify the repairs even more than we have already."

"Yeah? Well hanging around here didn't help them much, did it?"

Kate had to admit, Grimm had a point there.

"That's enough, Grimm!" Vickers snapped. "You're not helping."

Before Grimm could snap back, Decker intervened. He spoke in a much kinder, gentler tone. "Look, those guys on that tape were taken by surprise; they didn't know what they were up against. We do. We'll batten down the hatches, hold up tight, and wait for reinforcements." Decker patted Grimm on the back, and the scientist nodded back feebly.

"Now, do me a favor, start typing up a report on everything we've seen and experienced so far. By my count, we've got six people dead and one missing scientist. We are going to have to answer a lot of questions when we get back, and I want to make sure we've got some kind of written record."

"Okay, okay," Grimm replied. "And, sorry about earlier."

Decker squeezed the younger man's shoulder. "Hey, you only said out loud what we were all thinking." Grimm walked out of the room, his head low.

Before Decker could leave to begin fortifications, Kate and Vickers moved up to stand next to him.

Vickers was the first to speak. "Dex, how long before anyone realizes we're in trouble?"

Satisfied the three of them were alone, he answered, "As far as anyone knows, we were only conducting a possible murder investigation. My superiors wanted to keep everything out of the press, so I doubt most people even knew we were investigating a multiple homicide. There isn't any reason to suspect anything else would go wrong. As you know, getting stranded in the Arctic is not unusual for this time of the year. And even if anyone did know how much danger we are in, there isn't any way for them to reach us out on the pack ice during Phase III conditions."

"How long do storms like this usually last?" Kate asked. She immediately regretted asking for she wasn't sure she was prepared to hear the answer.

Decker tilted his head to one side and seemed to be sizing up her current mental state. "Could only be a few more hours, or maybe as much as a week. You just never know up here."

"Great."

Kate was right; she hadn't wanted to hear the answer.

Chapter 22

Grimm and Nikko

For the next three hours Detective Decker and Sgt. Jenkins strapped on their tool belts and went back to work shoring up their defenses.

Vickers began searching for any additional assets, like weapons. Kate wasn't sure what Grimm and Nikko were up to but after an hour of feeling like a third wheel, Kate decided to go back downstairs and see what other data she could glean from Sierra's research.

She was in the main lab searching through more of Sierra's notes when Grimm came briskly down the stairs. He was pulling on his Arctic jacket as he walked hurriedly towards the entry.

"Grimm, where are you off to?" she asked.

"I sure as hell ain't staying here," he said. Then he strode over to the exit, grabbed the hatch's handle, and started spinning the wheel.

Kate ran up beside him. "You heard Decker, we're not going anywhere in this storm. Besides, do you really want to go out there with that thing roaming around?"

Spinning the handle even faster, Grimm replied, "As opposed to what? Stay here and be a snack pack?" With a look of madness in his eyes he added, "You saw what it did to the wall. It already ate the two guards we came in with. We're no safer in here than out there. At least in the tractors we'll have a fighting chance."

"How do you figure? Those tractors are far less fortified than this building."

Grimm didn't answer. Instead he yanked open the hatch.

At that moment, Nikko came downstairs fully clothed.

"Nikko, will you talk some sense into Grimm? He plans on leaving in one of the tractors."

But Nikko strode right on past her without a word. Obviously, the two men had already discussed their plan, and they were now acting on it.

Grimm was about to follow the young native but turned back to her. "Kate, you're welcome to come with us. You're bat-poop crazy to stay here."

"Decker!" Kate yelled upstairs. "Decker, come quick!"

Grimm flashed her an expression of betrayal, and stepped into the arctic entry. "Fine. Every man for himself, then."

He turned to go out the door, but she grabbed him by his coat. "What the hell are you doing?"

"I'm trying to save your life." Turning her head over her shoulder, she yelled again for Decker.

"Let go of me, Kate." He wriggled out of her grasp with a shove that sent her sprawling to the deck plates. He hesitated for a second when he realized what he had done, but then moved back to the arctic entry. He didn't get far, though, because Kate heard booted feet clanging down the stairs.

By the time she regained her footing, Decker and Sgt. Jenkins had already sprinted by her and pinned Grimm against the wall.

"Where you going, Grimm?" Decker asked. "We're still in Phase III."

Before Grimm could answer, Sgt. Jenkins asked, "Where's Nikko, is he with you too?"

"Are you serious?" Grimm asked. "We've got to get out of here, man. You saw the tape."

"Where's Nikko!" Jenkins appeared ready to pop him.

"I told him to go outside and get one of the tractors ready. Now let me go."

Decker and Jenkins exchanged a worried glance.

Using the moment of distraction, and fueled by panic, Grimm shoved Jenkins into Decker. Both men cursed as they stumbled backwards over the bench along the wall. By the time they righted themselves, Grimm had vanished out the door.

Decker, the faster of the two, sprinted after Grimm and tackled him in the snow like a linebacker.

Sgt. Jenkins joined him and both men lifted a sobbing Grimm to his feet.

"You don't understand, we're in Phase III conditions," Sgt. Jenkins yelled to be heard above the wind. "This gale is strong enough to knock the tractors over. You'd be totally blind! Even if you made it off the island and back to the ice, you could fall down a fissure."

Grimm shook off the two men, and they released him. "I'm going, with or without you."

Sgt. Jenkins must've been tired of arguing because he walked up and punched Grimm in the face, knocking him to the ground.

Lying on his butt in the snow, Grimm felt his jaw and asked, "What the hell did you do that for?"

"You were going crazy. I was trying to knock you out so we could carry your butt back inside."

Grimm appeared stunned. When he spoke, his demeanor seemed less crazed. "Well, next time, if you're going to knock me out, then ... KNOCK ME OUT!" When the Sergeant stepped forward with his fist raised, Grimm nervously held up his hands and said, "No, no. Don't. I'm fine. I'll come back inside. Just help me up." He held an outstretched hand and both men took it and helped him to his feet.

"Wait a minute, what about Nikko?" Kate asked.

Decker stared at her. "What do you mean?"

"He went outside too," Kate yelled back.

Then they all heard it. A frightful roar, which was all the confirmation anyone needed.

Grimm did not wonder if Nikko was still alive. Instead, he ran back into the facility as fast as his spindly legs would carry him through the snow.

They heard a distant shotgun blast.

"Nikko!" Sgt. Jenkins yelled. He hefted his shotgun and headed out after him, Decker following closely behind.

When Decker turned his back to her, Kate was torn about what to do next: follow the men into the snow or turn back into the lab. Then she saw someone standing in the snow. The man was tall, much too tall to be Nikko, and he was certainly nothing like the creature they had seen on the video tape. His face was covered by a white mask and goggles, a parka hood pulled up over his head. He seemed unaffected by the storm, standing straight and tall despite the wind. Then he turned and walked away into the snow.

"Hey, you, wait!" she called out to him. "We need help!" She found herself chasing after the figure, but before she could pursue the strange hooded man further, something grabbed her roughly from behind. She let out a yelp and nearly jumped out of her skin.

Thank the Lord. It's only Decker.

"I saw someone," she pointed, "Out there, in the storm."

"Was it Nikko?" Decker asked hopefully.

"No, someone else, not one of us." When she saw Decker studying her face, she added, "I'm not crazy."

Decker shielded his eyes with his hands and stared in the same direction "I don't see anyone. Are you sure?"

Kate nodded, "I'm certain of it."

"I don't see anyone now." Turning back towards her, "C'mon, let's go find the others."

They found Sgt. Jenkins standing next to one of the three Arctic tractors. The tractor's door had been ripped off from the hinges completely, and the interior cab was splattered with blood.

The Sergeant finished checking inside the vehicle and then jumped back down to join them. "No one's in there."

"Maybe he made it back inside," Decker yelled.

"Man, I hope so," Jenkins answered, worried.

When the toe of her boot kicked something solid, Kate glanced down at her feet and thought she was going to be sick. "I don't think Nikko's inside."

Decker knelt down next to the severed arm lying in the snow.

When he lifted it up, Kate saw the hand was still clutching a shotgun. With some difficulty, he removed the weapon from the dead man's hand. There was a loud CRACK as Decker opened the cylinder and he put his nose close to the breech. When he lowered the gun away from his face, he said, "He managed to get off at least one round." There was a clinking noise as Decker hefted the brightly colored shotgun shells. "These are slugs." He turned to Kate to explain. "They're bear killers, not the usual ammunition."

"Didn't help Nikko much," Sgt. Jenkins complained sourly. Judging by his face, he clearly felt responsible for the younger man.

Decker must've seen it too for he told the Sergeant, "There's nothing you could've done." Decker put a hand on the Sergeant's shoulder. When Jenkins acknowledged him, Decker added. "Let's get Kate back inside."

The two men took up defensive positions to either side of Kate. Decker, grabbing her by her elbow, practically dragged her back toward the station.

As much as she wanted to retreat to the station, after they walked a few yards through the snow, she pulled her arm out of his grasp and said, "Maybe now that thing has eaten we should make a break for it."

Sgt. Jenkins shook his head. "I don't think it's gone. I think it's still here, close by."

Kate was scared, and turning her anger towards the Sergeant she said, "What do you know, you some kind of bear expert now?"

The Sergeant shook his head again, only this time he appeared even more frightened than a few seconds ago. He nodded grimly towards where they had picked up Grimm's shotgun.

Nikko's severed arm was gone. Only a pool of blood remained.

Chapter 23

Buttoned Up

Even though they were all tired, nobody could sleep.

The mood had been dour for hours now, and no one had wanted to speak about the monster outside, circling their base like a shark around a bleeding swimmer.

As it turned out, the Sergeant was first to break the silence with a found deck of cards. Vickers sweetened the deal by breaking open some snacks, and it wasn't long before they were all sitting around playing for peanuts; only Grimm was absent from the game.

The mood was lightening a little. Sgt. Jenkins was dealing the next round when he said, "Okay, okay. I got one. What do you call a wet bear?" When he was certain everyone was waiting for him to answer, he added with that big goofy grin of his, "A drizzly bear."

Vickers groaned. "Oh, that's terrible."

"You laughed, didn't you?"

"Like hell I did," Vickers shot back, but Kate thought she detected a smile.

"What do you get if you cross a bear with a skunk?"

"Give it a rest, Jenkins," Vickers warned.

Decker was still laughing from the last bear joke. Kate noted he had a nice smile. "No, no, I've got to know this one," he said, organizing his cards.

The Sergeant raised his eyebrows. "Winnie the P.U."

"Okay, that's kind of funny," Vickers reluctantly agreed. "Well, are you happy now, Decker?" When she saw his puzzled look, she added, "If that creature out there is any kind of indicator, it looks like there's still some magic left in the world."

Despite their dire situation, he grinned back. "Yeah, too bad it's trying to eat us."

"Seriously? Macho banter ... now?" Kate asked, jokingly.

"That's how we roll," Sgt. Jenkins said, grinning even more broadly.

That's when Kate knew these men were just as scared as she was. They just had a different way of dealing with it.

"I'm out," Jenkins said, throwing down his cards. Removing his hat and then replacing it, he asked, "Okay. What I want to know is, how would a ten-thousand-year old bear survive this long anyway, and how come nobody's seen it before?"

"Is it really so hard to believe?" Decker asked, shuffling his cards. "We've only explored a fraction of the Arctic. The Arctic Polar Ice Cap is twice as big as the United States. Other than the occasional commercial airliner cruising overhead at forty thousand feet, how much of it do you think is really explored?"

"Well, there are people living here, some native inhabitants. Somebody must've seen one in all these years."

Vickers took another card, frowned and then folded. "I'm sure they did, but they probably thought they were looking at just another polar bear."

"Or *maybe* it ate them," Decker added dryly. "You know how many missing persons reports we get in the northern villages a year?"

"Plus, if they're anything like polar bears, they probably spend an equal amount of time beneath the ice fishing as they do hunting on land above it," Kate added. "So it doesn't surprise me one bit they're out there." Then to Jenkins, "Two cards please, Sergeant."

"They, as in, more than one?" Jenkins asked.

Before Kate could respond, Vickers piped up. "Where there's one, there's got to be another, right? Mom, Dad, siblings."

"Okay, but why now?"

"Why, what now?" Kate asked, confused.

But Decker answered the Sergeant for her. "Probably for the same reason polar bears are moving more and more inland: depleted food source, shrinking ice packs. There's a reason polar bears are on the endangered species list."

"The Lazarus taxon."

The Sergeant switched his gaze from Decker to her. "Come again, the Lazarus-what-now?"

Kate grinned slightly. "It's a term that scientists use for a plant or animal in the fossil record that they thought was extinct only it turns up alive and well."

Vickers lifted her eyes from her cards. "Example?"

Kate shrugged. "Actually, there's dozens. The Coelacanth once swam with dinosaurs. We thought it was extinct along with them about a million years ago, that is, until one turned up in a fisherman's net off the coast of South Africa."

Decker chimed in. "Even mountain gorillas were thought to be the stuff of legend up until only about a hundred and fifty years ago."

"You're kidding?"

When Decker shook his head, the Sergeant removed his hat, scratched the peach fuzz on his head, and then replaced it.

"And don't forget that giant squid those Japanese scientists filmed a couple years ago. Even after whales were washing up on beaches with giant sucker markings on their skin, scientists still refused to believe in their existence."

"Well, I'll be ..." the Sergeant looked over at Kate and decided to keep the rest of his anecdote to himself. Instead he leaned forward and pretended to talk in a hushed tone. "Maybe it's like Jurassic Park? Maybe some scientists found frozen prehistoric bear DNA and cloned themselves a prehistoric bear." He gazed around the table before continuing. "And maybe we'll find a trashed up scientific laboratory where all the scientists have been killed where they had been conducting ..." the Sergeant stopped in mid-sentence when he locked eyes with Kate. "Oh, sorry."

Vickers shot the Sergeant a glance telling him that his joke was in poor taste.

Kate could tell Decker hated himself for asking, but ultimately he did anyway. "Kate, they weren't doing any research like that out here, were they?"

At first she thought he was joking, but when everyone grew quiet and was listening intently, she blurted out, "No, of course not." Of course, now she had to tell them what they did find.

C'mon, Kate, it's now or never.

"All right, Kate. You in or out?" Decker was staring at her evenly.

"Uh, what?" she asked nervously.

Did Decker know already?

"You want to raise or fold?" he asked her.

Oh, the cards. I'm such an idiot.

"I'm in. I'll see your ten, and raise you twenty peanuts."

Decker was reading her face. Kate could tell he thought she was hiding something. He leaned forward on his elbows, looked her square in the eye, and said, "I think you're holding something back." He then shoved all his peanuts into the pot. "I'm all in."

Sgt. Jenkins removed his hat and whistled aloud.

"Don't do it, Kate," Vickers warned.

Relieved, Kate ate one of her peanuts, smiled back at Decker. and pushed all her peanuts into the center pot. "Call, Detective."

Decker's nose crinkled when he smiled and he lay down two cards. "Two aces."

Kate noted that the Sergeant still hadn't put his hat back on.

"Sorry, James," she said as she laid her cards on the table. "Three Jacks."

Sgt. Jenkins let a loud cry and put his cap back on while she raked in the pot. "Better luck next time, Detective."

Kate wasn't sure, but as Vickers gathered up Decker's cards for the next deal, she thought she saw a third ace in Decker's poker hand. The two detectives shared a quick look but neither of them said anything about it.

Son-of-a-gun. He let me win.

Before she could say anything, the Sergeant asked, "Hey, Kate, what happened to all those Ice Age behemoths you were talking about, anyway? And what'd you'd call this place, Barren Gina?"

"Beringia," Kate repeated patiently. "About twenty-four thousand years ago, between North America and Asia, just on the edge of the Arctic lay an ancient place called Beringia. Because so much water was locked up in the glaciers during the Ice Age, this land connected the two continents."

The Sergeant tilted his head to one side. "Wait a minute, you're telling me that there used to be a land bridge between Russia and good ol' U.S.A.?"

Kate nodded. "That's not all. Even after everywhere else had frozen in the northern regions, ice glaciers never formed in Beringia because the climate was too dry."

"On the little land bridge between us and Russia?"

"Yes. In fact, Beringia was blanketed in hardy grasses, herbs, birch, and willows, supporting extinct species like the wooly mammoth, the mastodon, the steppe bison, the North American horse, the scimitar cat, the dire wolf, and of course, our ugly friend out there, the giant short-faced bear."

"Okay, okay, I'm tracking all that, but what happened to them? I mean, according to that ride down in Disney World, all the dinosaurs were killed off by a giant meteor, so what happened to *these* guys?"

"The end of the Ice Age was a time of catastrophic change. As the climate became warmer, glaciers in the northern hemisphere began to thaw, releasing immense quantities of water. Sea levels rose all over the world. Low-lying regions, including the nutritious grasslands of central Beringia, were flooded. With their food source gone, herds of grazing animals quickly vanished. The predators which fed on them, like the giant short-faced bear, quickly followed. With the end of the Ice Age, Beringia and the giants that once roamed there survived only in legend and deep in the frozen ground. Beringia was truly a land of Ice Age monsters. The biggest grazers and their most fearsome predators were far larger than any mammals that live on this continent today."

"And where does our short-faced bear rank amongst them?" Vickers asked. Her tone suggested she didn't want to know the real answer.

Kate's voice became solemn. "Like Grimm said earlier, it was the largest, most powerful carnivore among the Pleistocene land mammals of North America. Highly carnivorous, it preyed on even the largest of animals and was capable of killing a mammoth with one mighty swipe of its paw."

"Have you ever heard of anything like this happening before? I mean, an extinct predator attacking humans?" Decker asked.

"I've read eyewitness accounts of Inuit peoples who reported seeing living mammoths in Alaska; one tribe even provided drawings of the animal, but I never actually believed those stories. At least that is, not until yesterday."

After this sank in with everyone for a moment, Sgt. Jenkins got up from his chair and stretched. "Well, I don't know about you guys, but I'm beat."

The others got up and expressed similar sentiments. Kate found herself reluctant to turn in for the night without being fully honest with those who were sharing her fears.

"Wait!"

Well that had come out louder than I'd intended.

"I've got to show you guys something."

Kate led them downstairs and, before she could lose her nerve again, she showed them the map, the photograph of the jade totem, all of it. Kate had trouble reading his face, but Decker wore an expression of betrayal, although he said nothing.

"Remember when you said all we need to do is find the motive? Well, here it is."

"What are you saying, Kate?" Decker asked. "You think someone killed your friends because of this?"

"Don't you think it's strange that the moment that Eugene and Sierra Banks discover a dig site that clearly predates the Egyptian Pyramids by thousands of years, a prehistoric bear shows up and wipes them all out?" She shook the photo of the jade totem to catch his attention. "A discovery of this magnitude would, at the very least, change the face of archaeology forever. A ten-thousand-year-old artifact like this alone would be worth billions, if not priceless."

"Yeah, but Kate, you saw the playback. It was a giant prehistoric bear."

She nodded in agreement. "Yes, the bear was the weapon, but what about that man I saw in the storm?"

"What man?" Vickers asked. Then to Decker, "What man is she talking about?"

Decker answered, "Kate saw someone standing out in the storm."

Kate was relieved that he didn't use the word *believed*.

Vickers looked from Kate to Decker, and stared at him evenly. "Did you see him too, Dex?"

Decker hesitated before answering. "I called out and searched the area but no, I didn't find anyone." Then catching Kate's glare, he quickly added, "I guess he must've run off."

"In this storm?" Vickers asked. "Where could he possibly go?"

"Dunno. We were trying to find Nikko and that was our priority at the time."

Kate could see Vickers was working the angle out in her head. "So, you're thinking someone baited this bear here somehow to keep anyone from finding out about the dig site?"

"Exactly."

"What makes you think the guy in the storm didn't find the dig site already?" the Sergeant asked.

"Because they didn't have this," Kate answered, pointing to Banks's map. "They tore the place apart looking for it, but it was drawn on the back of the grease board the whole time."

"Not exactly clandestine," Vickers muttered.

"Sheer dumb luck they didn't find it," Jenkins added. "But it worked."

Decker scratched his head for a moment. "I guess there's only one way to find out. We've got to find this dig site of yours."

"I'm going with you, too," Grimm said.

Everyone jumped. Grimm had crept up on them so silently. She found herself wondering how long he had been there.

Decker raised an eyebrow. Grimm was the last person he'd ever think would join the little expedition. "Really, why?" he asked suspiciously.

"Hey, I'm not a coward, okay. That thing really freaked me out. But it's like Kate said, this could be the find of the century. You're going to need someone to document it." He held up his camera. "And I'm the best man for the job."

"All right. Unless there are any objections, with the exception of Vickers, who will call for the cavalry the moment the storm clears enough for the radio to get a signal, we all head out to the dig site in the morning."

Despite being on edge, Kate surprised herself with a yawn. Sleep deprivation was finally beginning to catch up with her. "Sounds good to me."

Around the room, the others nodded murmured agreements. Then they all dispersed to grab some rack time.

Except for Decker, who took first watch.

Chapter 24

The Stelae

"**According to Banks's** map, this is the place."

Following Kate's directions, Decker brought the big tractor to an abrupt stop in an oval clearing surrounded by rock face. He kept the engine and lights on and hopped out. "Okay, we walk from here."

When they had first left the research station, the storm had abated to Phase II. They had no way of knowing if Vickers had reached anyone from the mainland on the station's radio because on this side of the island, they were separated from the Spam Can by a large mound of mountain rock.

As the crow flies, the dig site was only a mere twenty miles from the Spam Can, but the windy road they had traversed had taken them three times that. They had passed through the whalebone graveyard and followed the shoreline just like on the map, but thus far all they had seen was various rock outcroppings on the left and crushing pack ice surrounding the island on their right.

Everyone slowly clambered down from the tractor tires and into the melting snow.

"Are you sure this is the right place?" Kate asked.

Decker took his GPS unit out of his pocket, wiped snow off the display, and said, "It's the same coordinates as on the map."

Sgt. Jenkins jumped down beside them. "According to the calculations, we should be practically on top of the dig site."

"Then, where is it?" Kate searched their immediate surroundings. "I don't see anything."

Sgt. Jensen turned towards the plateau to the left of the road. "Maybe up this hill?"

Decker took one last look around. "Okay, unless anyone has any better ideas, let's see what's at the top."

Kate tightened the hood of her parka against the howling wind. With her rucksack slung on her back, she followed them upwards.

It was slow going up the steep grade. For every three steps Kate took forward, she slid at least one back.

Three-fourths of the way up, she paused in a patch of snow as high as her thighs, and gulped some air into her burning lungs. She controlled her breathing as best as she could. *In through the nose and out through the mouth.* She wiped the sweat from her goggles with her sleeve, for the snow fog obscured her vision. The worst part was her burning nose and throat. No matter how much she tried covering them, they were always the most painful when she ran in the cold.

Seeing her lag behind, Decker came back down to her while Sgt. Jenkins helped Grimm up the rest of the way to the ridge.

Decker removed a canteen from his belt. "Here, drink some water. It's a lot easier to get dehydrated in the Arctic than people think."

While Decker gave her enough time to drink the bottled water, he readjusted her pack. "You need to keep your straps a little tighter, so your pack doesn't feel like it's pulling on your back."

She went to hand the canteen back to him but ended up dropping it into the snow. "Sorry. I can't feel my fingers anymore."

Decker removed two red packets out of one of the duffel bags and shook them like sugar packets. "Here, these are warm packs," he explained. "Put them in your gloves and you'll be toasty in no time." He then reached forward and pulled her hood up. "And try and keep your head covered at all times. We lose over 90 percent of our body heat out the top of our heads."

"Gee, thanks, Ranger Rick," she retorted and smiled at him.

She couldn't be sure because of the scarf over his mouth, but if his eyes narrowing were any indication, she assumed he was smiling back. She found herself wondering if he was still hurt from being betrayed.

If we ever get out of here alive, I swear I will make it up to him.

Decker recovered his canteen, and they began hiking upwards once more. The steepest part was behind them; the grade now seemed gentle by comparison.

She was nearly to the top when the Sergeant appeared on the ridge, shouting something indiscernible down to them.

"What is it, Sergeant?" Decker asked, holding a gloved hand to his ear.

Sgt. Jenkins cupped his mouth and shouted louder this time. "I said, I think we found something!"

It still took another ten minutes for her to reach the ridgeline, but when she finally staggered up onto the plateau, she immediately saw the cause for the Sergeant's excitement. The three men were standing next to an enormous modern, heavy-duty tripod. It was set up over a gaping hole. And next to the hole was a thick five-foot-tall limestone tablet sticking out of the snow.

Busily filming the stone column with his camera, Grimm asked, "What the hell is it?"

"Seems pretty old," the Sergeant said, running an ungloved hand over its surface.

Before she could answer, Decker added, "It reminds me of a road marker."

Kate studied the huge marker. She had seen similar ones near the Mayan temples on the Yucatan Peninsula.

"It's a stela," Kate answered. Then, seeing their confusion, she added, "It's like an ancient billboard. The Mayans had them; signs like these usually stood before a temple pyramid or pointed the way to a hidden tomb."

"See those dashes and dots?" When they all nodded, Kate explained. "The Mayans used bars and dots to express numbers and record time. In this case, a dot equals a value of one and a horizontal bar equals a five."

"So this is three?" Decker asked, clearly interested, and pointed at a crescent shape carved in the limestone.

"No, that's a crescent," Kate replied. "They are actually fillers. You have to be careful not to confuse those with dot numbers."

"You think Mayans are somehow connected to this stela found here?" Decker asked.

Kate smiled patiently at him and said, "Some scientists have been trying to prove that all races are linked by one ancient race, or mother culture, for the past hundred and fifty years. It's been my life's work for the last decade."

Sgt. Jenkins looked up suddenly. "Hey, you hear that?"

Then Kate heard it too. The sound of tent flaps snapping briskly in the wind.

"Over here," Decker shouted, finding the source of the noise.

Set up behind nearby rock formations, Kate saw a campsite consisting of two large tents.

They all trudged through the snow over to them. It was easy to see why the expedition had chosen the location for a campsite because as soon as they had cleared the rocks, they were immediately cut off from the worst of the wind. Sgt. Jenkins peered into the nearest of the tents. Not finding anyone, he checked back with Decker. "Think these belong to the man Kate saw in the storm?"

"Dunno. Camp looks like it's been deserted for a while, though," Decker muttered, releasing the flap of the second abandoned tent.

He was right. Chairs were thrown about, open containers of food lay empty, big red coolers were tipped on their sides, and several pieces of equipment were overturned in the snow.

"Let's head back over to the hole," Decker suggested.

The five of them knelt by the excavated hole, approximately five feet wide and shaped like a mouth. Decker cracked open a flare, making Kate jump. Phosphorous light glowed; he dropped it in and they watched it sail to the bottom.

Sgt. Jenkins lifted his gaze from the hole. "I'd say it goes down at least a good thirty feet. Let's check out the rig."

"What?" Grimm asked him. "You mean, we're actually going down there?"

Decker patted Grimm on the back. "We didn't come all this way for nothing."

The Sergeant and Decker inspected the auto winch attached to the heavy-duty tripod. There was a harness at the end of the cable. Decker hit a button and played out several feet of cable.

Sgt. Jenkins grabbed the cable and pulled all his weight against it. "Seems sturdy enough." He took another glance down the hole. "Any volunteers?"

"Count me out," Grimm immediately answered. When the other two men eyed him, the scientist added, "I don't do heights."

"I'm going," Decker announced, grabbing the harness.

Sgt. Jenkins wiped the fog from his glasses. "Maybe I should go, Dex."

Decker frowned. "You're the strongest of all of us. If it's all the same to you, I'd like you to stay up here so you can pull me out in case this contraption decides to quit working."

"I'll go," Kate heard herself say.

"Yeah, let her go," Grimm immediately answered.

"No way. Out of the question," Decker responded curtly.

"Why?" Grimm whined. "It's not like other scientists haven't already been down there already."

Kate laid a hand on Decker's. "I want to go. And, if this thing does break down, the two of you can pull me out a lot easier than the Sergeant can by himself."

Decker understood her reasoning; it made the most sense. Regardless, he stared at the ground, shook his head and said, "No way."

The Sergeant rested a gloved hand on Decker's shoulder. "She's right, Dex. Besides, if that thing comes poking back around, she'll be a lot safer down in the hole than up here with us."

"Yeah, Dex, he's right," Grimm said, then thinking about it for a moment he added, "Wait a minute, what?"

Chapter 25

Down the Rabbit Hole

Decker's large hands cinched the straps around her waist. A flush of heat ran through her body as he helped her into the harness.

"How's that?"

Groaning, Kate answered, "Ugh, little tight."

"Well, you want it a little tight so you don't fall out of it."

"We've got power." Sgt. Jenkins eyed Kate. He was holding the box that operated the electronic winch. "I'm ready when you are."

"Give us a sec," Decker grumbled. "Now, swinging out over the hole is the hardest part, but we've got you."

Before he could instruct her further, she immediately kicked off the side and dangled beneath the apex of the tripod and hung over the opening.

"This isn't my first rappel."

"Really? Do a lot of spelunking in your off time?" Decker shot back. He was clearly not comfortable with her going down into the hole first.

"I took a class at my gym," she answered sheepishly. Her body stopped its pendulum motion.

"Here you go, boss," Sgt. Jenkins said, handing him one of two heavy-duty, water-proof flashlights.

Decker flicked it on, and after playing the light beam over his forearm, he passed it over to her.

"Got it."

Sgt. Jenkins leaned forward. "Here. It's one of the radios I took from the research station. We're on channel one. We will be in contact with you the whole time."

Decker checked the carabineer on her harness one more time to make sure it was locked tight. "Once you get down, you can unhook yourself from the cable, but don't stray too far from the drop zone."

Kate flashed him a mock salute. "Yes, sir." She wasn't sure where this sudden rush of bravado was coming from. Perhaps it was adrenaline, or maybe it was the fact she was about to see the dig site with her own eyes for the very first time, or maybe it was just plain old fear. Most likely a combination of all three.

Decker nodded to the Sergeant, who depressed the big round button that started the winch.

The cable unwound smoothly and slowly as it lowered her down into the pit. She clicked on the flashlight that Decker had given her, and the ice crystals surrounding her danced in the beam of the light. As she descended, she ran gloved fingers over the icy walls. They were smooth to the touch; far too perfect to be shaped by hand alone. She wondered if the researchers had created the perfectly formed chute using boiled hot water.

Her radio crackled and Decker's voice came over its tiny speaker. "Kate, come in. Do you read me, over?" She fumbled for the radio, held it to her lips, and clicked the mic. "I'm about halfway there." She made a mental note to keep her breathing steady. Decker was worried enough as it was, and she didn't want him pulling her back up just because she was breathing heavily.

"Copy," replied Decker. "We're reading you loud and clear."

She pushed aside what might happen if the cable broke by thinking about what lay below.

Did Eugene and Sierra make it this far?

The memory of their loss panged her heart greatly. *Focus*, Kate told herself. *Now's not the time. You can serve their memory best by concentrating on finding out what they gave their lives for.*

When her feet touched ground, she stood up. She had some difficulty uncinching the straps of the harness, but when she finally did, she dropped it to the floor and stepped out of it. Her heavy clothes were so cumbersome that she nearly tumbled over doing it, but with her arms out for balance, she managed to regain her footing. Decker would probably have a fit about her unclipping herself, but it was the only way she could move about the cavern unhindered.

Surprisingly, the ground she stood on was not ice but mostly dirt, or more accurately, silt.

Seeing the cable was still spooling down into a coiling pile, she called upwards, "I'm down." Then realizing she should probably use the radio, she fumbled for it on her belt and brought it to her lips. She took a controlling breath and in as calm and professional voice as she could muster she said, "I'm down."

The winch switched off signifying they had heard her. "Copy. Remember, don't wander too far from the drop zone."

Yes, mother.

The wind howled in the opening overhead, but the lack of chilling wind was welcome. She unzipped her coat and threw back the hood. She also pulled off her mittens and stuffed them into one of her oversized pockets. The air smelled crisp, and puddles of meltwater splashed underfoot.

Kate remembered she had put the flashlight Decker had given her back into one of her oversized pockets. She fished around, found it, and switched it on. The light was not as bright as she would have liked, but she was able to scan her immediate surroundings a lot more clearly.

Kate turned in a circle, sweeping out with her light. She saw more evidence of other scientists: survey equipment, supply crates, candy wrappers, and perfectly shaped oval holes where they had dug frozen specimens out of the ice.

"Kate, you doing okay?"

It was Decker.

"Yeah, just looking around."

"What do you see?"

"Nothing interesting so far." She noticed a brand new generator connected to a light stanchion. "There's a generator down here."

"Fuel?"

She checked the gauge. "The generator's empty, but I see a barrel of fuel nearby. I'm going to see if I can't get it started. Stand by."

It took a few moments to refuel the generator by flashlight, but once she remembered how to use the choke properly, it rumbled to life on the third pull. Almost instantaneously, the light stanchion brightly lit up the room.

With the additional light, she noticed an entrance to a narrow gorge on the far side of the cave. The stanchion's power cord snaked deeper into the ice, like a breadcrumb trail beckoning her to follow. She shone her light down the tunnel. About twenty yards down the tunnel there was a bend, but she could just make out light emanating on the far side.

"There's more artificial lighting at the other end of a tunnel. I'd like to check it out."

"Copy, but stay in constant radio contact."

"Affirmative."

Decker's last transmission sounded more garbled than before, most likely due to the rock. She figured it would only get worse the farther she moved away from the opening above, making it difficult to stay in constant contact as Decker wanted her to. But she had to know more.

With her heart thudding against her chest, Kate ventured down the icy corridor. Wind whistled through the passage and chilled her to the core; she realized that there must be another opening.

She was nearly at the bend in the tunnel when she heard a small crumbling noise behind her.

Giant Ice Age Bear – Giant Ice Age Bear, her mind screamed.

She turned around and panned her flashlight behind her, but the beam of light revealed only an empty passage.

"Hello!" Kate called out.

The echoes of her words were the only answer.

Maybe Decker had followed her down here. She reached for her radio.

"Decker? This is Kate, do you read me?"

Static.

Damn.

Her mind was shouting at her to go back to the hole. She twisted back to the bend in the tunnel. *But I'm so close.*

In the end, curiosity drove away the fear, some of it anyway.

As she rounded the bend, the tunnel emptied into a large chamber about the size of a tennis court. The roof was dome shaped and covered in stalactites pointing down like jaws ready to clamp down and shear her into pieces.

There's a cheery thought.

From the threshold, Kate struggled to make sense of what she was seeing. There were stone blocks scattered about the cave and even more half-submerged in the ice. Goose bumps pimpled her arms; these blocks weren't just stone. They were hewn block, in other words, carved by stone cutting tools!

The sound of waves lapping brought her attention to a small pond. She could smell the salt, and guessed it was connected to the ocean. Kate adjusted the nearest light stanchion to reveal the far wall.

Is that an actual building?

The light revealed an archway made of stone that reminded her of the pillars of Stonehenge. Kate noted strange symbols inscribed on the granite posts. Her heart beat rapidly with excitement. She stared at the blurred writing. Her heart ached to study what was written there, but she had more immediate concerns.

Further evidence of the scientists was scattered everywhere. Another generator sprouted power cords snaking out to the light poles at every corner. Small red flags peppered the rocky cliff face. Piles of sample bottles cluttered the cavern floor; surveying strings divided the floor into sections with cordoned off pathways between them.

Kate was afire with the thrill of discovery that had been part of her chosen vocation since she had first decided on her major of archaeology. This place was an archaeological goldmine.

Kate carefully picked her way through the cavern and stopped at the pond separating her from entrance to the ancient ruin. Kate theorized that the warmer water must have been what made a natural cavern around the dig site.

She was about to see if she could start up another generator and turn on more lights when she realized that Decker was probably going ballistic on the surface by now. Kate brought the radio to her mouth to try once again to reassure him, but no words escaped her lips.

The beam of her flashlight revealed an object in the shadows. Tilted on a slant almost identical to that of the Tower of Pisa was a ten-foot-tall jade totem in the center of the room. The ancient artifact was beyond valuable. And like more modern totem poles, this one also told a story. Starting at the top of the column, the first pictograph depicted a man with squiggly lines coming out of him. The squiggly lines were aimed at a menacing bear that was facing him. In the pictograph below it, a man was holding something to his lips and pointing to another group of men. The third pictograph needed little interpretation; the bear ripped the enemy into pieces.

What did it all mean? It is almost as though the guy with the squiggly lines coming out of his head is commanding the bear to attack his enemies.

She moved closer to the base of the totem, hoping to see more detail, and then she saw something slumped up against it.

It was a frozen corpse.

She backpedaled out of the cavern and ran back down the corridor. But the harness she had used to descend was now vanished.

What the hell? Why did they reel it back up?

She fumbled for her radio and prayed that it would work. "Uh, Decker, could you come down here, please?" Her voice trembled.

Thankfully, Decker's voice came back over the radio. "What is it, Kate, what do you see?"

Kate swallowed before she spoke, and then said, "I think I found Eugene Banks." Then remembering the story on the totem, she added dazedly, "Oh, and you should probably bring your gun."

Chapter 26

Ruins

"Oh, Eugene. I'm so sorry."

"Did you figure out cause of death yet?" Grimm asked, watching the scene unfold on the digital display of his camera.

Decker looked into the lens and gave him a stern glance, "Give us a minute, will ya, Grimm?"

Kate was kneeling next to Banks's body. "No, no, it's okay. I want people to know what happened here."

Decker shrugged.

He had only given Banks a cursory examination, but he couldn't find any obvious signs of foul play. "There's not a scratch on him. Near as I can figure, he just laid down right here and froze to death."

Fighting tears, Kate asked, "Why didn't he just leave? It makes no sense?"

"Not sure. Grief, maybe?"

"Or maybe something scared him so bad he was afraid to leave," Grimm offered.

"No. I don't think that's it." Turning to Grimm, Decker asked. "What position was the winch in when you and Sgt. Jensen first found it, up or down?"

Grimm thought about it for a second, "Um, up, I think."

"Why?" Kate asked.

On the playback, we saw Banks leave the station by himself. If he came here and lowered himself down, how'd the harness get winched back up?"

Kate raised an eyebrow and answered evenly, "Somebody stranded him down here."

"The man you saw in the storm, was it Banks?"

Kate flashed back to her memory of the man in the storm. "No. Eugene's jacket is red. The man I saw was wearing a white parka and he was a lot, lot bigger."

"And you're sure it wasn't a..." Grimm began.

Cutting him off, she answered curtly, "I know the difference between a bear and a white parka, Mr. Grimm."

While Decker continued his investigation, Grimm walked over and stood on a small beach next to the pond. At his feet were the fossil remains of a large-sized creature lying half in and half out of the water.

Kate yelled after him, "Grimm, get away from that water!"

"Why, it's obviously dead." Grimm retorted, kicking the bones with the toe of his boot.

"Because I said so, that's why," Kate scolded. "Who knows what other monstrosity is lurking about beneath the water." After everything they had seen so far, it was easy to imagine some frightening water creature lunging out of the small pond and snatching up Grimm in its array of multi-toothed jaws before wriggling itself back into the inky depths. They had no idea what other kind of indigenous carnivores might have survived ... and that included in the water.

Ignoring her request, Grimm offered, "Bones are too big to be human," and continued filming.

"Polar bear would be my guess," Decker explained, joining them.

But Kate didn't hear him; she was too busy studying the wall across the small pond. Most of the ruins had long since collapsed, but one section of the wall looked solid enough, the exposed section looking like the remnants of a lost city swallowed up in an ocean of frozen sea long, long ago. She noted that the exposed parts of the brooding temple had a charcoal-stained reflective surface that resembled sculpted lava rock. At the structure's center was a pyramid-shaped roof surrounded by four towering obelisks that stood guard on each corner, like long forgotten stalwart sentinels.

"Any theories on what we're looking at?" Decker asked, stepping up beside her.

Kate nodded in response. "At first I thought it might be some sort of tomb, but do you see how reflective the surface of the temple is?" When Decker nodded, she continued. "What a lot of people don't know is that the Great Pyramids of Egypt were originally built with the same polished limestone block coverings. The light of the sun reflected off the pyramid and could be seen for vast distances, theoretically even from orbit." Kate had to force herself to keep her voice steady and calm. "And the Greeks believed that the north countries were cold because of the breath of Boreas, the north wind. They believed that beyond the Boreas were warm and sunny lands, where the sun shone twenty-four hours a day. Maybe one day long ago, they were actually right."

"I heard that people refer to Beringia as the Atlantis of the North." He glanced over to her and grinned.

"Sounds like someone went to my Arctic symposium."

"Not really. Vickers downloaded it before we left Deadhorse. I must admit, I wasn't buying any of it either, until just now."

"Yeah, you and three other people make four who believe in my theories." The memory of the president of Iceland cruelly dismissing her theories still panged her. *I can't wait to smear what we've found in that bastard's smug face. They'll be a lot more believing in me now.*

Decker shined his flashlight at an area hidden in shadow. "Kate, is that an entrance in the center?"

Decker was right; on the front façade she could just make out a visible entrance. There were two lofty columns on either side supported by double entablatures. The temple ruins had suffered badly from erosion, and the relief sculptures had been almost completely destroyed, but the entrance still seemed accessible.

"We've got to get over there somehow," Kate exclaimed, feeling her pulse quicken.

Decker studied the water between them and the ruins. He knelt down next to the pond and put his hand into it. Judging from his reaction, it was much colder than even he anticipated. "This water is glacial melt water; we wouldn't last five minutes in there without a dry suit."

Grimm joined them. He was still filming with his camera when he said, "I don't think you guys want to swim in that."

"We could just walk across the water," Kate offered.

Both men turned to look at her as though she had gone insane.

At first she hadn't seen any way to negotiate the pond either, but then she had spied stones hidden inches beneath the water's surface and grasped the builder's original intent immediately. If primitive man were to witness someone crossing the lake from afar, it would appear as though the person were walking on water. *As though he or she were a god.*

"What are you talking about? I don't see anything," Decker stammered, frustrated.

Kate stepped up on a rock outcropping behind Decker, grabbed his head in her small hands, and turned his head towards the hidden stones, "Over there, silly."

"Oh, I see them now."

"Those clever little bastards," Grimm breathed excitedly and then stepped forward and zoomed his camera on the ruins across the pond. After a moment of recording he added, "I don't like the looks of that place; you sure you want to go in there? Most likely it will collapse on you guys the moment you set foot inside."

"You're more than welcome to stay out here, Grimm," Kate said, failing to keep the disdain out of her voice.

"I plan on it," Grimm spat back. "And you should stay, too. With that thing running around. I'm just saying that if you two want to risk your necks, go right ahead, but I'm staying out here."

Decker intervened. "That might not be a bad idea," he said to her. When he saw her look of displeasure, he quickly added, in a calm and soothing voice, "If the structure does collapse on us, Grimm will be able to dig us out or at the very least direct a rescue party to our remains."

Grimm nodded. "Besides, I've got plenty to document out here."

Before she could step onto the hidden bridge, Decker grabbed her by the arm. "Hang on a second." Turning towards Grimm, Decker removed his Glock from his holster and offered it to Grimm.

As Grimm took it, he accidentally hit the magazine release button and the ammo clip dropped to the dirt. The skinny scientist picked up the dropped magazine.

Seeing Grimm's look of uncertainty, Decker asked, "You were in the military; you do know how to use one of these, right?"

"We only shot rifles in Basic," he answered sheepishly. "And I'm strictly a forensics criminologist, not some common patrolman."

Decker recovered the Glock and magazine. He blew the dirt out of the dropped magazine before inserting it back into the pistol.

Holstering the Glock, he removed a second pistol from his pack. "Here, try this instead. I took it from the armory back at the facility," he said, handing Grimm a revolver. "It's a Taurus. But be careful. There's no safety, so keep your finger out of the trigger guard until the front sights are on the target and you've decided to shoot. It's loaded with bear killers and packs quite a punch."

Grimm nodded. "Okay, I doubt I will need it down here, but thank you."

"Oh, and make your way back to the hole and be sure to let Sgt. Jenkins know what's going on. And tell him we might not be alone out here, so stay on guard."

"Copy."

Decker joined her at the pond. Fortunately, the boots that the Sergeant had first outfitted them with would insulate them from water as well as the cold. Moving carefully, one stone block pedestal step at a time, they walked across the small pond and reached the entrance.

Kate was about to go inside when Decker stopped her. "What are you doing?" When she tilted her head with a puzzled expression, he added, "Don't you remember what happened back at the facility?"

"Still not following."

"How about you let me go first?"

She nodded in sudden understanding. Decker raised his pistol and entered the dark stone tunnel. Stopping just inside the entrance, he turned back towards her. "I don't suppose there's any way I could talk you into staying here while I go and check things out first and make sure it's safe inside?"

She shook her head and answered, "Not in a million years."

Decker suppressed a grin and said, "Okay then, let's go." He flicked on his flashlight and went inside.

Kate paused for a moment when she found herself staring at Decker's boots. Pure white sand spilled amongst several roughly hewn temple blocks on the floor nearby, marking the spot where the original survey team had first broken through the outer wall. *This is it,* Kate thought. *This is where past meets present, where my conception of history changes forever.* There was so much to discover. She had so many questions.

She took a few more tentative steps into the opening, waved back at Grimm still filming her, and then entered hallowed halls that hadn't been negotiated in over ten thousand years.

Chapter 27

The Map

Picking their way through the rubble and fallen debris, Kate and Decker passed through a central doorway whose crossbeam was adorned with a frieze of triglyphs and metopes.

Kate pointed out the niches on either side of the doorway. "These niches probably contained statues in a distant past." As they continued onward, Kate noted the numerous façades carved out of the rock wall; they reminded her of the Nabatean ruins of the Jordan. Kate whispered, "The architectural skill we are seeing here easily transcends the Incas."

At the end of the short corridor they now occupied, she saw a short flight of stairs that led downward. After descending the steps, Kate and Decker entered a long, dark corridor on a lower level. The walls were slick and cool to the touch.

Their flashlights probing the darkness, they moved forward. Kate followed Decker. For such a tall, broad-shouldered man, he negotiated fallen columns and cracks in the floor with relative ease. She fought the urge to examine every nook and cranny of the place, promising herself to return one day and explore the site thoroughly.

Kate noticed that the granite floor was pocked with occasional holes, perhaps where the ancient temple had succumbed to earthquakes, glacial movement, or simply the wear and tear of time. In either case, the holes were not a good sign, especially since she guessed they were already another thirty feet beneath the ground. Caught up in the excitement, she pushed the memory of Grimm's earlier warning aside.

Per his survival training, Decker pulled a glow stick out of his pack and dropped it on the floor to mark the direction they had come. It would be easy to get lost in the maze without the lighted trail. If the place did start to collapse, they would want to find their way out in a hurry.

After a few more minutes of walking, Decker stopped before three corridors. "Which way now?" When she didn't immediately answer, he was about to take a step down the middle corridor when Kate abruptly stopped him with a hand on his elbow. "Not that one," she said.

"Why not?" he asked, disgruntled, probably because she had startled him a little.

Kate raised her flashlight to an overhead symbol marking the doorway. It was a drawing of a cloaked man poling a ferry boat. "See that symbol there?" When Decker nodded, she continued, "The Greeks had something similar. It means path to the afterlife."

"Ah," Decker replied. The corridor to the left had succumbed to a cave in. "What about this one?" he asked, illuminating the adjoining passageway to the right. The symbol above this doorway resembled a half-open eye.

Kate studied it for a moment. "That one looks more like the Egyptian symbol for Ra, the sun god. In this case, it probably signifies the path of enlightenment."

"Well, Dr. Foster, I don't know about you, but the path to enlightenment sounds a whole lot better than the path to the afterlife."

"Agreed."

Decker led them carefully down the path of enlightenment, both unaware that Kate had spared his life as well as hers from a concealed, spring-loaded trap hidden in the floor.

They walked down the sloping hallway in silence. The air was crisp and stale at the same time. Several times they had to slosh through water, but the depth was rarely above their ankles. About halfway down the long, sloping corridor, Decker could see an antechamber up ahead on the right.

"Kate, I think I see an alcove."

She opened her mouth to answer but was suddenly overpowered by the harsh odor of death.

This new chamber was rectangular and about the size of an average garage. It was as empty of antiquities as the rest of the temple, but what was immediately apparent was the pile of ravaged corpses within. Half-eaten bodies lay everywhere: skulls, femurs, ribs, all splintered, cracked, and gnawed upon. A terrifying shudder shook her by the spine. The smell of multiple pools of blood, bowels, and excrement on the floor was overpowering.

"Bear den," Decker muttered. "Now we know where all those missing persons from the villages disappeared to."

Kate grimaced at the sight of the ghastly bloated faces. She fought the vile stench permeating her nostrils and the bile creeping up in her throat. "There's more over there," Kate choked out, gagging from the smell.

When he swung his light to illuminate the back wall, they saw more unmoving crumpled forms with their intestines hanging out of their abdomens.

Heart pounding in her chest, holding her scarf firmly over her mouth, Kate found her attention caught by one of the half-eaten bodies who seemed familiar.

"Oh no," she moaned. "I think this one is Sanjay."

"We need to go."

"No, no. I'll be okay."

"You don't understand. We need to go." Decker pointed to the large track on the floor. It resembled the massive bear track they had seen back at the facility. "I think we're in its den. Most bears don't like fresh meat. This is probably where he stores his victims to rot awhile."

Kate could only nod in reply. When Decker saw she was about to lose her lunch, he came over to her and helped her stand. "Try concentrating on breathing through your mouth." When she composed herself and nodded to him that she was all right, he swallowed heavily, fighting the bile rising up in his own throat. "C'mon, let's get out of here before whatever did this comes back."

Every fiber in her being wanted to leave this place and never return. But what she saw drawn on the wall covered in splashes of blood was no less than astounding, and stopped her in her tracks.

"James," she said. "Wait."

She shone her light on the drawing on the back wall. Above the pile of corpses, they could just make out a map. It depicted several continents, but not in their modern-day forms.

"All the continents are joined together by a single landmass in the Atlantic," Kate exclaimed. There were also faded pictograms of pyramids in a place labeled Aegyptus, as well as an area that might be the Yucatan Peninsula; there was another pictogram of something that looked akin to the Tower of Babel in the Middle East. Sri Lanka was connected to India and even the poles seemed to include cities the size of which could only be possible in ice-free lands.

"Do you think this is some sort of ancient map?" Decker asked.

"Precisely," Kate breathed. "I think we are looking at a map of the earth before the last polar shift."

"How do we even know this map is accurate? I mean, maybe it sprang from some artist's imagination?"

Kate smiled. "Do you see on the map where Antarctica is clearly drawn?" When Decker nodded, she continued, "That shoreline is fairly accurate, just like the Piri Reis map."

"Wait a minute. You lost me. What's a Prairie Rice map?" Decker asked, confused.

"Piri Reis map," Kate corrected. "In 1513, a Turkish Admiral collected maps from all over the world so that he could draw his own."

"Wait a minute, are you talking about the sailor who claimed his source maps were found in the ancient Library of Alexandria."

In her excitement, Kate interrupted him. "The historical importance of this map is that it demonstrates an ancient knowledge of an ice-free Antarctica drawn by a pre-Ice-Age civilization."

"Hey, check out Alaska," Decker announced.

Kate could see that an outpost was drawn on the northwest section of the Alaskan Peninsula. The Bering land bridge was nearby and connected North America to Asia. She could also see other cities mapped out in Africa, the Middle East, Florida, and the Yucatan Peninsula.

"One thing's for certain. This map is why Eugene and Sierra Banks were here. It is literally a window back in time to an age of an ancient mother culture."

"I guess we now know why they call this the path of enlightenment," Decker mused.

"Wait a minute. Did you hear that?" Kate asked but before he could answer, they both felt the ground shaking beneath their feet.

"The floor!" Decker shouted at once.

Before she could react, he grabbed her roughly and shoved her into the doorway. The floor fragmented beneath his feet, then gave way entirely.

Even if she had not been paralyzed by fear, Kate would never have reached him in time before he plunged into the unknown depths below.

The collapse was over as quickly as it had begun and she found herself utterly alone in the den of human carnage.

Dropping to her knees by the hole, she shouted into the darkness below, "Decker!"

The feeling of dread that danced up and down her spine was magnified tenfold when she could just make out a low guttural growl originating below.

She retrieved her dropped flashlight and shined it into the hole. "Decker, where are you?"

Scaring the life out of her, a hand shot up out of the hole and grabbed the edge. "Will you get that damn light out of my face and help me up?"

"Oh, thank God, you're okay."

She was about to put the light down and help him up when she saw something in the dark below Decker. There was no mistaking the prehistoric monster for its descendant. Its head was massive, and the bear's burning red eyes made it seem more like a hound of hell than anything from this world or its past.

Voice tempered with fear, she stammered, "Ba ... Ba ... bear!"

A huge roar motivated both of them to get Decker out of the hole. Getting back to their feet they glanced once more down into the hole.

"Do you think he'll jump?" Kate asked him, frightened. Although she couldn't see the rest of it, she figured there was no way that thing was going to fit through the hole.

Decker grabbed her by the hand. "I sure as hell don't want to find out," he said, and led her back towards the entrance.

They made a mad dash back down the corridor, staggering out of the crumpling entrance as the temple ruin collapsed behind them. They negotiated the pond bridge as quickly as they dared, reached the other side, and dropped down to their backs to catch their breath.

"Do you ... do you think ... do you think he got out, too?" Kate asked between gulps of air.

Chapter 28

No Return

"**Good news, weather's** clearing. Soon as we get back to the station, we're getting the hell out of here."

"You don't have to tell me twice," Grimm radioed back. He returned to the first chamber and could just make out Sgt. Jenkins's silhouette gazing down at him from up top.

"If you don't mind, I'm going to go warm up in the tractor for a few minutes. While you guys have been poking around down there all morning, I've been up here, freezing my ass off."

"Okay, no problem. Decker and Kate are still in the ruins. I'll check back with you … say, on the hour?"

"Copy that," he heard the Sergeant reply through what sounded like chattering teeth.

Grimm signed off and returned to the main chamber. When he did, he saw Kate and Decker crossing the last few feet to shore. "Well, speak of the devil and the devil appears," Grimm muttered to himself. Then he noticed the urgency in their movements as they strode quickly towards him.

"We're leaving," Detective Decker announced in clipped tones.

"Sure, once I'm done digitally processing this room," Grimm replied.

"No time, we've got to leave right now," Decker said, as he began quickly collecting gear and roughly stuffing what he could into his backpack.

"Why, what's wrong?" Grimm asked. "What did you see over there?"

Kate opened her mouth to speak but found she couldn't talk. Decker answered for her. "All you need to know is we're getting out of here right now."

Grimm didn't seem to hear Decker. Instead, hands trembling, Grimm reached for the pistol tucked in his belt and pointed it right at Kate.

Finding her voice, Kate asked, "Grimm, what the hell do you think you're doing?" *Is Grimm some sort of saboteur?*

But then Kate heard a bubbling sound emanating from the pond. She suddenly realized that Grimm wasn't pointing the gun at her; he was pointing it at something behind her.

Fear gripping her tightly by the abdomen once more, Kate forced herself to turn her head back towards the pond.

The skull of the creature slowly revealed itself as it rose out of the water. The mouth split open wide, revealing a maw of sharp teeth.

Focused on getting to the winch to the surface, Decker was unaware.

BOOM!

Kate jumped at the sound. Grimm must have squeezed the trigger because the muzzle had erupted in a deafening roar. He was shaking so uncontrollably that he completely missed the bear with his first shot, which was truly surprising since there was so much mass of the bear to hit. Instead, he ended up putting a deadly slug into the ground only two inches from Decker's left boot. When Decker glared back at him, Grimm stared back at him, wide eyed.

"What the hell, Grimm?!" Decker shouted angrily, but then he saw the expressions on their faces. He spun around swiftly towards the pond.

The thing was monstrous. They were trapped. Her breathing grew faster. The cavern seemed to close in around her.

Before they could retreat, the bear charged out of the water. Both Decker and Grimm trained their pistols in that direction. He and Grimm each fired a hail of bullets upon it, but it barely slowed the monster down. The bear recoiled from each hit but seemed unhurt; if anything, it just pissed him off. "Reloading," Decker yelled, hit the ejector, dropped the spent magazine, and inserted a fresh magazine, all in about a second. The bear shook off the hits. "No effect," Decker said aloud, more from training than for anyone's benefit.

As he reloaded with practiced hands, Kate could see they were only delaying the inevitable. Their pistols were incapable of puncturing the bear's thick hide.

Decker snapped another magazine home, pulled the trigger, and hit the bear square in the snout, blowing off a chunk of it.

Still the bear lumbered towards them.

Decker only had time to turn his chin toward her and yell, "Kate, run for the corridor," before the bear slammed into him so hard that Kate feared the impact had killed him instantly.

She waited for Grimm to fire his revolver again, but he just stood there, staring up at the bear with a horrified expression.

The bear's clawed hand struck Grimm so hard that the lanky scientist's upper torso snapped around to face the cave behind him, tearing his spinal cord in half in an instant. Kate could only watch, shocked, as Grimm's broken body crumpled onto the cavern floor. The pulpy mess writhed around for a few more seconds and then was still.

While the bear patted around Grimm's corpse, Kate saw Grimm's dropped pistol lying in the sand nearby. Before she knew what she was doing, she recovered it.

Slowing her breathing, she stared down the sights of the revolver and aimed at the thing's head, now lowered into Grimm's eviscerated stomach.

CLICK.

Despite her fear, she remembered Grimm had fired off one round at Decker and only three at the bear. She remembered James telling Grimm that the pistol held six shots, so the gun should have three rounds left. *What the hell happened?*

She clumsily cracked open the revolver's cylinder and dumped the shells onto the cavern floor. She saw four spent shells and two good cartridges. With shaking fingers, she picked the two good bullets out of the sand and inserted them back into the cylinder.

She risked a quick glance at the bear and was horrified to see the bear was now watching her, staring at her with a quizzical expression.

Kate snapped the cylinder closed.

The bear didn't like that sound. He raised his body onto his hind legs and let out a gigantic roar.

She knew she was dead.

Seemingly from nowhere, Decker sprang in front of her. He was waving a makeshift torch at the bear.

"Kate, get the hell out of here!"

She would have liked nothing better, but the bear was now between them and the only exit.

Decker must have realized this too, for he shouted, "Get back!"

Kate was unsure whether he was shouting at her or at the bear. He was still waving the torch in front of him, but she knew it wouldn't hold off the monstrosity for long.

She scanned the room quickly; the only other avenue of escape was across the pond and into the temple, but even if it hadn't collapsed, she was well aware what lay at the end of that grisly road.

Kate turned back towards Decker in time to see the bear smack the torch out of his hand. It flew through the air and landed in the pool of water.

The bear wasted no time, advancing on Decker. It reared back its mighty paw, just as it had done with Grimm only seconds earlier. Kate knew Decker's death would be just as instantaneous.

But instead, Decker had the sense and quick reflexes to pick up a wooden crate lid lying at his feet and used it as a shield when the bear struck him. He still flew across the cavern like a flailing human Frisbee, but there was a chance he might still be alive.

Decker landed a good ten feet away. Fighting to rise to his feet, he fell back to the ground. The bear lumbered towards him. This time the monster was going to finish the job.

"Over here!" she shouted. *What the hell am I doing?*

All the bear's focus switched back towards her. She slowly backed up a few steps, but then tripped and fell onto her backside.

Really?

Scrambling backwards, much the way Eugene Banks must have done, she found herself with her back to the jade totem. She must have bumped Banks's frozen corpse because his head lolled on his neck and turned towards her as if to say, "See, this is how I died, Kate."

But why didn't the bear eat him?

Banks had been defenseless. She stared at the ancient amulet he had strung around his neck; her senses sharpened by desperation, she found herself staring at the little holes in the shell. *Like a flute.* Then she looked at the pictograph of the man holding something to his lips and commanding the bear to attack.

And that's when it came to her. Was it possible that this pre-Neolithic race had somehow found a way to domesticate the giant bears? The pictograph certainly seemed to suggest so. There was no reason to believe that the flute work on the bear now, to believe that it had recently been thawed from the ice, or would still respond through some kind of genetic trait that had been passed down through millennia.

The bear let out an exploratory bark as it circled like a shark, closing in for the final kill.

She grabbed the seashell and pulled. The leather string snapped and she held it in her hands.

The bear was right in front of her now, reared up on its hind legs, and towered over her much the way it had with Grimm and Decker, its paw raised to strike. Her mind went numb as she stared up at the bear, now on all fours, right in front of her. The thing was far too massive for the modern world.

The prehistoric monster studied her too. Jaws smacking, lips rippled back to reveal all its massive teeth. Its breath reeked of foul carrion.

With what she feared would be her last breath, she feebly blew through the shell and a strange whistling flute noise came out of it.

The bear stopped its ferocious growl and gazed upon her like a dog trying to understand television. It turned its head to the side and sniffed her for a few seconds.

Her life story didn't flash before her eyes and she didn't have any epiphanies or regrets, but she did realize that she still clutched the pistol in her right hand.

Kate knew she had only two rounds, but the weapon had failed her before. It was like Russian roulette, but with slightly better odds of two out of six.

As she raised the pistol, it was lucky that the barrel was already pointed up into the inquisitive bear's face. The bear sniffed the end of the barrel. All she had to do was squeeze. Kate summoned the little remaining courage left to her and jammed the barrel into its probing maw. The bear sensed Kate's change in energy. Its gums retracted and a deep ferocious growl escaped its maw, building in tempo. When her finger yanked on the trigger, the barrel was completely in the bear's mouth.

BANG!

The bear's head flew back from the blow. It stood up on its hind legs in rage, howling, shook its head and toppled over.

For a few minutes, she just lay there, shocked that she was still alive.

"Over here."

It was Decker, thankfully not dead. He raised one arm, painfully, to signal her.

Kate dropped the flute necklace around her neck and crossed over to him to help him stand.

Obviously in excruciating pain, he managed to ask her, "You okay?"

What a stupid question considering the circumstances. She was light-headed and electric jolts of pain shot up and down every muscle in her body, but she answered, "Just peachy."

Her knees trembled and she fell against him, hugging him. He was all muscle and bone. He let her sob into the folds of his coat for a while and then said, gently, "Hey, what do you call a bear ballet dancer?" She couldn't answer. "A bear-a-rina."

Despite Decker's poor attempt at copying Sgt. Jenkins's humor, and her own pounding heart, Kate cracked a teary-eyed smile.

"C'mon, let's get out of here."

They turned to start towards the exit, and only then noticed the men in white parkas. They were all holding automatic rifles, and they were all pointing the weapons straight at them.

Kate realized she had left the revolver with the one remaining round back by the totem, and Decker was out of ammunition entirely.

"Aw, crap."

Chapter 29

Here Comes the Calvary

Rifle barrels leading the way, four heavily armed soldiers in Arctic BDUs, with machine guns strapped across their chests, now faced them.

A thin, dark-skinned soldier stepped forward. Decker's sharp eyes caught the name Stimey stenciled onto his overalls. "Please, nobody move." Stimey's accent sounded Sudanese. Decker noted the man was missing at least three fingers. He wondered if Stimey was a refugee from the ongoing civil war that still ravaged the country of Sudan.

After the initial shock of seeing the armed men, Kate seemed overwhelmed with relief. Decker could see she was still shaking from her encounter with the bear, but with these soldiers to protect them, their chances of survival had increased exponentially.

"Give you people a lift?" came a loud commanding voice from the gorge entrance. Decker turned toward the newcomer who was the last one to enter the chamber. He was easily as tall and broad-shouldered as Sgt. Jenkins. But where the Sergeant was a bit younger and had a boyish looking face, this man had a storm-ravaged face, hair as white as snow, and a humorous squint in his bright blue eyes. Unlike the hardened soldiers securing the area around them, he did not wear battle fatigues nor carry a rifle, only a holstered sidearm. This new guy was clearly as dangerous as he was big.

After recovering his composure, Decker asked, "And you are?"

"Name's Major Barauch," he said as he hopped down from the ledge by the gorge to land beside Decker. "Me and my boys were training with the Arctic warriors when we picked up your distress signal."

Decker took the Major's outstretched hand and shook it. "I'm James Decker, and this is Dr. Kate Foster."

But the Major didn't appear to have heard him. Instead, he shook his head in awe at the sight of the enormous creature behind them. He walked past them, removed an insulated glove, and stroked the hair of the dead monster. "Boy, he's a big sucker, isn't he?" He turned back to face them. "You guys are lucky to be alive," he added in what probably sounded like a slight Russian accent to most people, but Decker had traveled abroad enough to know it was Yugoslavian.

"Not all of us made it." Decker said solemnly, then remembering Jenkins, he asked, "I've got a Sergeant topside, he okay?"

At this, Barauch's tone immediately grew more serious, "I'm sorry," he answered, then nodded towards the bear, "I think your friend over there got ahold of him before we arrived."

The timeline didn't make sense, but Decker, tight-lipped, only nodded.

"Either of you require medical attention?" the Major asked.

Decker glanced over to check Kate before answering. "We're both a bit bruised up, but we're sure glad you showed up when you did."

A field medic wearing glasses stepped forward and started giving Kate a cursory examination. The medic removed a penlight and, with the practiced moves of an EMT, he examined her lacerations. Putting the penlight in his teeth, he removed a small can from his vest, shook it, and then began spraying down her lacerations, the medicine cooling her wounds almost instantly.

"Are there any other survivors down here with you?" the field medic asked her through clenched teeth, still biting down on the penlight.

"No, we're all that's left," Kate answered, sadly.

The medic checked to see if the Major had heard her answer, and then removed the penlight from his mouth. "Okay, that should stop the bleeding until I can get the boys back down in Fairbanks to stitch you up. I've treated you with some topical antibiotics. I can give you some painkillers too, if you like."

Kate simply shook her head.

Barauch's eyes widened at the extent of the claw marks on Decker's jacket. "You'd better let one of my men check you over, too, Mister ..."

"Decker," he said reminding him, but, wincing in pain, he waved the medic off.

Seeing this, Kate strode forward. "Don't let him fool you," she said, turning Decker's back toward him, "That thing smacked him clear across the cavern."

"How'd you know we were here?" Decker asked.

"As I said, we got a mayday from your research facility. Your pal, Vickers, wasn't it? Anyway, she said we ought to come out here straight away and gave us the coordinates."

Decker's eyes narrowed. *Uhmmm ... yeah, sure buddy.* The missing fingers, the variety of nonstandard combat issue weapons, the accents: none of this was adding up. "You guys aren't really with the Arctic Airborne Infantry, are you?"

"I have no idea what you are talking about, Mister Decker," the Major answered in broken English, with a crocodilian smile, his stare equally venomous. Clearly, this was a man not used to being questioned.

"Okay, let's start over," Decker said, as he removed his wallet badge and flashed it toward the Major with his left hand, keeping his weapon hand free, although at the moment, he didn't even have a weapon. "I'm Detective James Decker with the Alaska Bureau of Investigations. Let's pretend that for the past twenty years, part of my job was to interrogate people and know when they are lying. So let me ask you again, who the hell are you people?"

Before the Major could answer, there was a loud crash as two more men dropped a crate onto the ground. Although they were both huge, their size was the only thing they shared in physical appearance. By the looks of him, the

Pacific Islander standing to the left of the crate was at least four hundred pounds. His mouth hanging open was a sure sign of the man's vast intelligence. His partner had close-cropped blond hair, bright blue eyes, and a thick square jaw, much like the Major's. He wasn't as tall as the Major, but the fabric of his uniform strained from his muscles underneath.

Ignoring Decker's questions, the Major introduced the two newcomers. "Detective Decker, this here's the finest Arctic Airborne Ranger there is, Sergeant Vladislav Shevchenko."

The big blond stepped forward, clasped Decker's hand, and crushed it in his own grip. "You can call me Vlad, like the Impaler."

This got a chuckle from the big Samoan.

"Just call me James," Decker replied, "Like the Saint."

Decker noticed the big Pacific Islander staring at Kate with an appreciative eye. Shaking off his initial surprise, Decker asked sarcastically, "Are you an Arctic warrior, too?"

The beefy soldier walked over to stand before him. His shoulders were easily twice the width of Decker's. He looked down at Decker with a menacing stare and grumbled, "No, I'm the Ferryman," he said with an equally thick Islander accent ripe with sarcasm.

The Slavic Major, a big blond musclebound guy who was obviously Russian, the skinny Sudanese guy, a four-hundred-pound Pacific Islander, and a field medic with glasses. These guys were obviously not standard army, but mercenaries. Most likely they had gotten wind of the jade totem somehow and had been hired to retrieve it.

The five of them made the odds five to two, and one of those two an untrained female scientist. Decker knew he should have been intimidated. But he wasn't. He had been through far worse in combat oversees and patrolling a beat as a police officer. "Okay, we can either do this the easy way, and you can answer my questions. Or we can do this the hard way. Trust me, I don't think you're going to like the hard way."

The Major ignored Decker completely; instead he told the big Pacific Islander in a calm voice, "Shoot him."

Kate cried out, "What?"

The oversized Samoan raised his AK-47, took aim at Decker's chest, and pulled the trigger.

Move you idiot ... move. But Decker didn't move. He was like a deer in the headlights. It had all happened so fast and unexpectedly. He had been out of action for far too long. And now it was too late, for the big lummox had already squeezed the trigger. After all they had survived, it was a simple bullet that was going to take him out.

CLICK

At least he wasn't the only one to make a rookie mistake today. The big guy had forgotten to chamber his first round. The big man realized his mistake and with a curse, reached for the slide.

"Dammit, Finau," the Major cursed, and then unholstered his personal sidearm.

Decker heard the distinct sound of the AK-47 chambering its first round, but this time he did move. He grabbed the field medic standing next to him and maneuvered the surprised mercenary in front of him just as the Major pulled the trigger of his pistol.

BANG-BANG-BANG-BANG!

The medic convulsed as the hot lead slammed repeatedly into his body.

As the man went limp in his arms, Decker reached for the medic's holster. He expertly flipped off the retention strap with a flick of his thumb and removed the guard's sidearm. From the feel of it, Decker guessed it was a 9mm Glock. Dropping the dead medic to the floor, he aimed his stolen pistol at the Major, Stimey, and the four-hundred-pound Islander. "Now, drop your weapons," he ordered.

Shocked by recent events, the three mercs froze before him, but none of them dropped their guns.

"I said, drop your weapons," Decker ordered a second time with more fervor. He was only dimly aware of someone moving up behind him.

Wait a minute, where's the fourth guy, the blond Russian?

Off to his right he heard someone say, "Night-night, sweetheart." This was immediately followed by a thump on his skull and ...

... the world just went away.

In the growing blackness, the last words Detective Decker heard were, "Alright, bring me the girl next."

Chapter 30

Phone Call

"What now?"

"She's just extra baggage, kill her," Major Baruch said dismissively with a wave of his hand. He had crossed the dig site and was now studying the jade totem.

When the big blond mercenary snatched her by the arm and started yanking her towards the pool of water, Kate screamed. She tried to resist the man dragging her, but she might as well have tried resisting an angry forklift.

The musclebound merc forced Kate down to her knees by the pool of water moating the temple. His intent was clear; he was going to blow her brains out execution-style, and the pool would become her watery grave.

She was surprised to find that she was still holding the oversized flashlight Decker had given her earlier and realized she must've grabbed it when she and Decker had tried to leave the dig site.

When she felt the barrel of the Major's gun press against the back of her head, she dropped the flashlight into the pool. Her eyes followed its descent downward. In a way, it was kind of beautiful, the way the white hot beam reflected off the small water crystals floating in the water. She was mesmerized by the floating sparkles, not a bad last sight of the world. And then she saw the flashlight's beam illuminate the perfectly preserved alabaster stairs below the surface.

There is another antechamber below this one! And by the looks of those stairs, it's enormous!

The cruel irony was not lost on her. Seconds before a bullet was about to pass through her brain, she had found a secret entrance to an ancient site. Who knew how long before the entrance would be discovered again, if ever. These idiots' only concern was the jade totem. Didn't they know the totem was nothing compared to the map in the bear den? She couldn't even begin to imagine what other priceless relics might be lying at the bottom of the pool.

Oh, if only she could have returned with a team of divers wearing dry suits and vacuumed away the sediment to reveal the treasure, the antiquities underneath. Kate figured this was as good a last thought as any. She pushed away all thoughts of James Decker and the life she was only just realizing she may have had with him.

"Any last words?"

The big blond mercenary sounded surprisingly tender, for a guy who was about to blow her brains out.

Kate wanted to say something cool, or brave, like they always do in the movies, but with lips trembling, tears rolling down her cheeks, a shake of her head was all she could manage.

"Sir!"

The shout startled her so much that Kate practically died of a stroke, saving Vlad the Impaler a bullet. They both turned to see the skinny Sudanese guy, Stimey, now holding a computer in his hands, moving rapidly towards the Major, motioning for his attention. He showed the image on the screen to the Major. "You've got an incoming call."

Kate idly wondered how they were getting a signal but then glimpsed a portable relay station and antenna near the gorge's entrance.

When the Major took the computer from Stimey, Kate immediately recognized the man's digital image on the computer screen. *Ragnar Grondal, that son-of-a-bitch. I should've known he could be behind all this.*

"Mr. President, we've acquired the object."

"Well done, Major," President Grondal replied, in his usual precise Icelandic accent. "I want that totem and any other relics you can find crated up and on the chopper by nightfall." After a second's thought, he added, "Oh, and bring the bear." As though speaking to someone else off screen, he said under his breath, "It will look good in my private collection."

"Understood, sir."

"Demolition the dig site, but I want to interrogate Dr. Foster personally."

"And the bodies of the others?" Stein asked.

"Bury them along with the dig site."

Hearing this, Vlad the Impaler yanked her to her feet. "It seems you have a stay of execution, Dr. Foster."

Finally finding her courage, she ripped her arm out of Vlad's grasp and spat back, "Aren't I the lucky girl."

He took a step towards her, clearly intending to strike her. Kate immediately shrank away. But before he could subdue her again, the Major ordered, "Quit screwing around and get her back to the surface." Then turning to the other two men, he added, "Stimey, Finau, start rigging up the explosives."

With Vickers back at the research station and everyone else dead, Kate knew nothing could save her now.

Chapter 31

Blow Up the Dig Site

Get up, Dex.

Every muscle in Detective Decker's body was raw. *No, I don't want to play anymore.* He felt dried blood on the back of his skull where that cowardly S.O.B. Vlad had cracked him over the head earlier.

No, Decker concluded, he didn't want to play anymore. He'd done his job; he had figured out what had killed the scientists and what their motive was in doing it. No reasonably sane person could ever have predicted the Ice Age predator they had faced, or these damn mercenaries trying to recover the artifacts.

Against his body's wishes, Decker forced his eyes open. He was lying face down in the dirt. There was a loud buzzing in his ears, and when it began to subside, he heard voices. For a moment, he forgot where he was.

Stimey's high-pitched voice yelling from across the cavern was a harsh reminder. "Damn it, Finau, I said hurry your fat ass up before they leave without us!"

"I'm not fat," Finau responded patiently, "I'm just big boned."

The shrill voice again. "Let's go. We are leaving."

"Give me a minute. You want these things to blow up while we're still trying to get out of here?"

"Do you really want the Major to come back down here? Or worse, Vlad?"

"Almost there ..."

"That's it, I'm leaving without you," Stimey threatened, and when Decker slowly lifted his head, he saw the Sudanese mercenary do exactly that and dash into the narrow gorge exit.

Unflustered, the big man finished with whatever he was working with, rose mightily off of his haunches and lumbered towards the exit ... leaving his AK-47 leaning on a crate.

As Decker moved stealthily towards the forgotten assault rifle, he saw something on a crate nearby that made his eyes widen: a blasting cap wired into dynamite, a AA battery for a power source, and a digital timer that was counting backwards. These were the four components of an IED, the kind of improvised explosive devices he'd seen many times before. According to the timer, there were only five minutes and thirty-five seconds left.

They're going to blow up the damn dig site.

The moment of distraction proved to be detrimental. While he was studying the IED, Finau slammed into him like a linebacker. The tackle carried them both across the room and ultimately sent Decker tumbling over another set of thick wooden crates.

Ugh. As if my body wasn't hurting enough already.

In his younger days, Decker might have expertly tucked and rolled on the other side. This time, however, his thighs had caught the edge of the boxes, and he collapsed in an ungraceful heap on the floor amidst several freshly broken artifacts. Seeing the fragments, he quickly thought, *Kate's going to kill me.*

Both men scrambled to their feet. The big Islander easily outweighed Decker by at least two hundred pounds. Decker was sure he would be unable to win in a fair fight, so before the big man could get all the way up, he jumped off the crate and kicked both feet into his face. While he was still stunned, Decker quickly threw several punches to Finau's meaty face. The big Islander took the blows and rubbed the fresh trickle of blood from his jaw. Then he chortled deeply and fixed Decker with an icy stare. Decker knew a killer when he saw one.

Using one of the wooden crates for support, Finau rose to his feet and towered over him. Decker punched the big man in the gut with two uppercuts. The big Islander chuckled again, unfazed.

"I don't suppose talking it over is an option."

In answer, Decker felt two oversized hands grab him by the shoulders in a crushing grip. Finau lifted him off his feet with the strength of a crane and growled, "I'm going to pull you apart with my bare hands!"

Ten years ago, Decker might have been able to give the big guy a run for his money. But Father Time was catching up, and less time in the gym, and more time behind a desk, only compounded the problem.

It was time to cheat.

"Yeah, well you're going to have to do it with one frickin' eye," Decker responded. He reached up with one finger and poked the big Islander in the eye with as much force as he could muster.

With a cry of anguish, the big man dropped Decker. But before Decker could dance out of the way, Finau backhanded him with a blow that felt like he had been smacked across the face with a two-by-four. Decker hadn't even recovered when Finau grabbed him by his jacket and tossed him across the chamber for the second time today.

Sheesh, I hope I get frequent air miles.

This latest flight landed Decker atop the stove surrounded by camping equipment. Stars flashing before his eyes, he blindly searched for a weapon, a knife, a gun, anything to combat the other man. His hands closed on the handle of something, but Decker couldn't quite see what it was. He felt Finau's two thick hands grab the clothes on his back and he was hoisted into the air to be thrown across the dig site a third time.

This time, Decker landed near the IED. He glimpsed the digital timer that read four minutes and seventeen seconds. If the big mercenary didn't beat him to death, the explosives would surely kill them both.

The big man's giant hands encircled his neck and picked Decker up off the ground by his throat. The Islander's leering face was close to his. "Good-bye, Detective Decker."

As the world faded away Decker croaked back, "Good-bye," then he swung with all his might the heavy frying pan he still clutched in his right hand.

WHANG!

The heavy giant released his grip and took a step backwards, with a confused look on his face.

WHANG, WHANG, WHANG. The pan clanged upside the Islander's head in rapid succession. Like a video game character that had just been beaten, the towering giant teetered for a moment, then fell on his face.

Decker risked a glance at the timer. They had less than four minutes. His foot kicked a pistol on the floor. Retrieving it, he snapped it back into his holster and half-stumbled toward the exit.

Three minutes, five seconds.

As he was about to enter the narrow gorge, he heard Finau groan behind him.

Aw, hell.

Moving back over to the big man lying semi-conscious next to the dynamite, he shouted in his ear, "C'mon, buddy, wakey-wakey."

With Decker's help, the big man woozily got up to his knees. Decker grabbed him by the arm, tried to run for the door, and was immediately yanked back onto the floor. The Islander hadn't so much as budged.

Man, this guy is really trying my patience.

"Pal ...WE ARE GOING TO DIE!" he shouted into his ear.

"What?" Finau responded groggily, but at least he was trying to rise this time. Decker ducked under the big man's shoulder and helped him to his feet. It felt as though he were squatting two tons of dead weight. "C'mon, big guy, you've got to help me here, left foot, right foot, left foot," he grunted, moving them both towards the gorge.

In James Decker's mind, he and Finau ran out of the chamber and leapt out the opposite side of the gorge as the cavern exploded behind them. Sadly, the reality was that they shuffled past the ticking time bomb like two old men living in a retirement community for the ancient. When they finally made it to the entrance of the gorge, a last glimpse of the clock told Decker that they now had less than two minutes.

Dripping with sweat, Decker had somehow made it back to the hole. A steel basket was waiting for them. Decker figured the mercs must have assembled a much larger rig to haul the totem and dead bear out of the dig site while he was unconscious.

"Hurry up, Finau," Stimey shouted down to them. The merc was far enough away that he didn't notice Decker half-carrying the big man.

Decker maneuvered them both into the basket and waved Finau's meaty arm up at Stimey and the winch started almost immediately. Halfway to the surface, Decker guessed they had less than sixty seconds.

Once topside, Decker half-carried Finau off the lift, but found the dark-skinned soldier pointing his revolver at them.

"You there, don't move." Clearly Stimey had not expected anyone other than Finau to emerge from the hole. "What did you do to Finau?"

Decker, still heavy with Finau's meaty arm over his shoulders, responded incredulously, "What did I ... do to him?"

Clearly unschooled in the ways of sarcasm, Stimey asked, "Yeah?" and then thinking aloud, "Is someone else down there with you?"

Thinking fast, Decker nodded toward the open hole. "Yeah, you got us, my crew is still down in the hole. Oh, and we disarmed your little bomb by the way. So ... that's not happening."

Stimey flashed Decker a look of disbelief. Not taking any chances though, he covered them with the pistol and moved carefully over to stand next to the hole. Decker, still aware the bomb was about to go off, shuffled discreetly away, trying to get as far as possible from the hole.

Seeing this, Stimey ordered sternly, "I said, don't move."

"Okay, okay," Decker said sheepishly. He watched as Stimey glanced down the hole. Decker thought he could just make out the sound of an alarm clock going off, which was impossible, of course, and dropped himself and Finau to the ground as a massive explosion emanated from underground and flew up the chute. Stimey, standing next to the open hole, was blown off his feet in a fiery ball.

Ears ringing, covered by debris and by Finau's body, Decker had been protected from the worst of it. He slowly crawled out from beneath Finau's unconscious form on his hands and knees. When his vision finally began to clear, he saw that Stimey's burnt corpse had landed a good ten yards away in the snow.

"Sorry, pal."

Hearing the sound of helicopter blades, Decker shoved Finau the rest of the way off him, stumbled to his feet, and moved towards a nearby ridge. About halfway there, he tripped over something half buried in the snow. He had landed next to the still form of Sgt. Jenkins laid out on his back. As he brushed more of the snow away from the Sergeant's lifeless face, Decker could see Jenkins's head lying in a small pool of his own blood. Decker pressed two fingers to the Sergeant's throat. There wasn't a pulse. As he dusted away more of the snow, further inspection revealed that the Sergeant had been shot multiple times in the chest, and his throat had been slit from ear to ear for good measure.

Those sons-of-bitches!

As much as he wanted to escape and bring back reinforcements, Decker knew that to leave Kate with the mercenaries was to sign her death warrant. Retreating was not an option. He'd never left a man behind and he sure as hell wasn't about to leave Kate Foster to these monsters.

Not wasting another second, he ran down the path toward the ridge. Peering over the rocky outcropping, he saw a twin-bladed aircraft parked in a makeshift landing zone cleared out on the ice field below. Decker recognized the aircraft immediately. It was a CH-74 twin-engine, tandem-rotor helicopter, more commonly referred to as a Chinook.

Scanning the soldiers and the cargo, he saw the dead prehistoric bear on a nearby pallet, as was the jade totem strapped down under a loose-fitting tarp.

But where the hell is Kate?

He was about to take up another position when he saw her. She was bound at the wrists and being forced up the ramp by two more mercs that Decker did not recognize. Kate ducked her head to shield her eyes from the debris being kicked up from the rotor's wash and vanished inside the aircraft.

He was about to make his way down to the makeshift airport on the ice when he heard someone clapping their hands together. Glancing over his shoulder, he saw Major Baruch and his attack dog Vlad standing behind him.

"Well, aren't we the plucky hero," Baruch mused.

Decker slowly raised his hands up and turned slowly to face them. Before he could even think about drawing the pistol he had picked up in the dig site, Vlad lunged forward, took it from him and tossed it away.

"Bind his wrists, and make sure he doesn't have any other weapons on him," the Major ordered.

As Vlad bound his wrists with zip ties, Decker contemplated jumping him. Even on his best day, he doubted he could take the muscled, obviously well-trained mercenary, and with the Major covering him, it was suicide.

"We're taking him with us?" Vlad asked.

"Yes, we're taking him with us."

"Really?" Vlad asked, confused. "All the way to Grondal?"

"No. I thought we'd drop him off along the way."

Vlad just smiled knowingly.

Hands tightly bound, Decker was led by Vlad down to the landing zone. By the time they had reached the aircraft, the remaining cargo had already been stowed.

The rotors were accelerating rapidly as Vlad roughly shoved Decker up the ramp. He, Vlad, and the Major were the last to board the massive helicopter. The hatch wasn't even fully closed when it began to take off.

As Decker felt the massive aircraft rise, he knew in his heart they were as good as dead, but at least he was on board with Kate.

Chapter 32

Aboard the Chinook

"You're bleeding."

Decker lifted a hand to his forehead and, wincing as he did so, felt the dampness there. "Just a scalp wound. It looks worse than it actually is."

So like him, Kate thought. It was bittersweet that he was still alive because she knew she was only going to lose him again.

The mercs had tossed them into chairs that were little more than haphazard cargo netting stretched across the metal poles lining the payload compartment.

Kate didn't mind admitting to herself that she was scared. Facing down the prehistoric bear had been terrifying enough, but now they were about to be executed by ruthless mercenaries. She stared at the cause, the jade totem. So much death surrounding it. Everyone at the facility who had died: Eugene Banks, Sierra, Sanjay, the intern Charlotte, Sgt. Jenkins and his three security guards, and now she and James were soon to be added to the long list. She wondered what the original builders might have thought about their creation being the root of so much senseless violence. Would they have simply smashed it to pieces? She certainly would have.

Beside her, James began working on his bonds.

Ever the optimist.

Making sure the guards were out of earshot, she murmured, "What do you think they are going to do with us?"

"Kill us, most likely," Decker responded. He had found a piece of bent metal in the fuselage's framework and was sawing away at the zip tie binding his wrists, all while watching their captors.

Kate nodded in agreement, but replied, "Geez, you couldn't have sugar coated it a little?"

Decker stopped for a second and gazed back at her, studying her. "I'm sorry, did you want me to lie?"

"Yeah," she responded in a harsh whisper. "Next time we are captured by ruthless mercenaries, you betcha, lie your ass off."

This got a chuckle from James. "Don't worry," he said reassuringly. "We're not dead yet. The bear, now that was scary. These guys? They're just paid thugs." He returned to sawing at his bonds, and in only a few more seconds, the zip tie broke free. He checked to see if the mercs had heard the loud SNAP, and once he was sure they hadn't, he began working on hers.

"Keep watching them, and let me know if they start over this way."

Kate nodded, trying to keep her wits about her. Decker's confidence was infectious and a small part of her believed they might get out of this in one piece. And why not? Like Decker said, they'd survived the attack of a prehistoric monster.

The moment her bonds snapped free, she immediately lowered her gaze and rubbed at her wrists. But even if she had been watching the guards at the back of the plane, this new threat had come from between two cargo containers.

"What the hell do you two think you are doing, huh?"

Both she and James looked up and saw a mercenary they had not seen before. He was on the short side, Hispanic, with a heavily pockmarked face, and was pointing a machine gun at them. "Hey, boss, over here!"

When James rose to the balls of his feet, the merc brought his weapon to the ready position and said, "Uh, uh, I wouldn't do that if I were you. I'll waste you right here."

Vlad and Finau, only a little worse for wear after their fight, joined him.

"I'm sorry, the captain hasn't turned off the fasten your seatbelts sign," Vlad said, with a smile like a shark's.

"Where exactly are you taking us?" Decker asked.

Vlad thought it over for a second, as though deciding if she were worth wasting his time. "Well, Kate has a date with her good friend Grondal in Iceland, but sorry, Detective, you only paid for half way."

This got a chuckle from the pockfaced guard. "You want me to tie them back up?"

"No," Vlad answered, staring Decker down. "I think this is far enough."

He punched a nearby button on the fuselage with his fist. A warning klaxon sounded and the ramp lowered, allowing torrents of wind to gush in. Their intent was clear; the mercs were going to toss Decker out of the Chinook during midflight.

"Sorry, amigo, nothing personal," said Pockmarks. "My pop was a cop too, you know? Even got him some shiny decorations for his service. Worked his whole life, only to end up as a security guard in a bank during his so-called retirement. I tried it, didn't take."

He pushed Decker towards the open ramp.

Kate was too in shock to move. It was all so surreal, almost as unbelievable as their fight with a prehistoric bear.

"Hey, what are you doing?" Vlad asked. When Pockmarks looked at Vlad questioningly, Vlad held up a harness connected to a safety line. "You want to get sucked out with him? Put your damn harness on."

"Safety first," Pockmarks said, smiling.

"Hey, where's my harness?" Decker asked.

At this, Vlad's eyes lit up brightly and he let out a guffaw. Patting Decker on the back, he said, "Hah, I like this guy, the intrepid hero right to the end." His smile became more venomous. "Sorry, my friend, no harness for you."

Decker nodded. "Go to hell."

"You first," Vlad answered. Shouting to be heard over the gushing winds, Vlad asked, "I don't suppose you will just walk out the back?"

"Yeah, c'mon, man. Don't be a wimp," Pockmarks goaded.

"Why don't you show me how it's done?" Decker responded.

"Finau, throw him out," Vlad ordered.

"No good deed goes unpunished, eh, Finau?" Decker asked him.

The big Islander looked at him sheepishly, shrugged his shoulders, and said, "Sorry, it's just a job."

As Finau shoved him towards the exit, Kate found her nerve, leapt to her feet and shouted, "Leave him alone."

The Hispanic mercenary spun towards her and violently butted her in the stomach with the stock of his assault rifle.

Before she could collapse to the floor entirely, the guard moved behind her and, cupping her chin tightly in his hand, spat into her ear, "Oh no, chica. I want you to watch while we toss your pretty boyfriend out the hatch."

Kate struggled to free herself from his grasp, but he gripped her more tightly. Satisfied she wasn't going anywhere, he then licked the side of her face with a long, slow lick.

Kate felt the bile bubbling up from her stomach. She was helpless and she knew there was nothing she could do.

Finau was still pushing Decker towards the opening maelstrom. Already, Kate could see the winds threatening to pull him off his feet at any moment.

"C'mon, Finau, push him out already," Pockmarks yelled jubilantly.

Finau gazed back at them with an expression of fear. In that single moment of distraction, Decker moved in a blur of speed, spun on the giant, and kicked out his knee.

"Oh crap," Pockmarks cried out, as his pal Finau fell to the ground, and Decker used the big man's forward momentum to swing him towards the opening.

The overpowering sucking winds did the rest. Poor Finau stumbled a few steps toward the open cargo door and slid the rest of the way down the ramp, where he was ejected out the back.

"Holy crap, man!" Pockmarks cried out loud, laughing hysterically. "Finau just got sucked out the back!"

Vlad simply shook his head. When he saw Decker moving towards him, he leveled his pistol at him.

Decker hiked his thumb towards the open cargo door and said, "I guess he forgot to wear his safety harness."

Vlad lunged forward, spun Decker around, and started pushing him towards the exit. When Decker resisted, Vlad kicked Decker behind one knee, forcing him to the ground.

Leering, his face next to hers, the Hispanic guard holding her said, "Don't worry, chica, it will all be over soon."

Vlad placed the gun to the back of Decker's head.

Kate couldn't watch and looked away. The man she could have loved, spent the rest of her life with, was about to die.

And there wasn't a damn thing she could do about it.

Just as she was about to close her eyes, she caught movement out of her peripheral vision. Someone, or something, was moving in the shadows behind the crates.

Kate saw red eyes in the darkness. It was the same red eyes she had seen inside the temple. An image burned forever in her mind.

It was the bear. And he was very much alive. But how was that possible? She had put the barrel of the gun right in the creature's mouth and pulled the trigger. A passing thought flashed through her mind; she remembered hearing about suicide attempts where people had shot themselves in the head and yet, impossibly, they still survived. Neither she nor Decker had checked the bear for a heartbeat. And this thing was easily ten times larger than any human. If anything, she had probably just pissed it off.

A low guttural rumble came from the shadows, steadily rising in pitch. Instinctively, her hand had risen to her chest, and her fingers felt something tucked beneath her shirt.

It was the bear flute. She had forgotten she was still wearing it. She still wasn't entirely sure how or why the flute had some sort of controllable properties over the bear, but she just didn't care anymore.

Oh, you bastards are gonna get it now.

Chapter 33

Crash Land

— Exact coordinates: Unknown

"Hello? Is anybody alive?"

The pain-racked voice echoed amongst the Arctic winds. It was the voice of a man who knew he was about to die.

When Decker first regained consciousness, he found himself in complete darkness and felt as if he couldn't open his eyes. *Am I blind?* He wondered. The rancid smell of burning flesh greeted his nostrils. It was a smell he had never gotten used to.

When the loud ringing in his ears finally subsided, he heard the crackling of a nearby fire, a steady howling wind in the background.

As he regained more of his senses, he felt blistering icy wind sting his cheeks. A sharp piercing sensation in his shoulder forced him to open his eyes. His gaze was immediately drawn to the metal strut protruding through his right shoulder.

Well, that's not good.

He cried out again, "Somebody help, I think I'm hurt."

Detective Decker winced in pain when he touched the wound, covered with frost. He was now grateful for the numbing cold because he realized it was the only thing that had kept him from bleeding out while he lay unconscious.

Must've gotten flung here in the crash.

He looked around trying to orient himself. The darkness about him was lit by several small flickering fires, and bright Arctic moonlight shined through multiple cracks in the shattered fuselage. As he became more aware of his surroundings, he realized that Kate wasn't anywhere nearby.

Decker neither felt motion nor heard engines roaring. The mighty Chinook, or at least what was left of it, was grounded.

Did we crash?

The last thing he remembered was Vlad and the other commandos trying to shove him out the back. Oh, and the bear. And some kind of strange music, like from a flute ...

Kate!

Decker tried to move, but cried out in anguish once more.

"Kate," he shouted. "Anybody? I'm hurt pretty bad here." The cold blistering wind that blew through the cracks in the fuselage was his only answer.

Turning to his left, Decker realized that someone was sitting beside him. He reached up and grabbed the guy's shoulder. It was Pockmarks, the one who asked him to walk out the back of the helicopter in midflight. Decker gave a sharp tug on the man's jacket and said, "Hey buddy, I'm hurt pretty bad here," but the mercenary's head lolled toward him on a broken neck and revealed a disfigured face with one eye popped out of its socket, still hanging by the optic nerve. Even though Decker was hurt badly, he realized that he had fared far better than the mercenary sitting next to him.

As his eyes adjusted more to the light, Decker glanced around at the cavernous interior. He realized with horror that there were twisted and broken bodies littered all around him, most wrapped in the cargo netting amongst the wreckage.

Am I the only one left alive?

"Kate!" he cried out again.

Where is she? Did she survive the crash? Please, God, let her have survived the crash. I can't do this again.

Decker knew he would need help soon, or he would join the ranks of the dead mercenaries.

His cries for help ignored, Decker reached up and attempted to pull on the metal rod protruding through his shoulder. Summoning all his strength, he slowly pulled at the pole that had speared him like a fish. Frozen ice crystals of blood crackled and made sickening sucking noises that were soon drowned out by his screams of anguish.

For his effort, he was rewarded with sharp pangs of lightning that danced up and down every inch of his body. Warm fresh blood leaked down his chest, and the world tilted a little crazily. As the echo of his scream died out, he realized the metal rod wasn't coming out of him because the shaft was still attached to the Chinook's fuselage. He knew that as soon as he removed the pole sticking through his shoulder, or to be more accurate, himself from the pole, he would most likely bleed out in a couple of minutes and die. Scanning the cargo hold, he was searching for something to clot the wound when he spied something even better.

The onboard medical station module was intact. It was only a scant ten feet away, if only he could get to it. Of course, there was always the danger of passing out before he could staunch the wound, but since clearly no help was coming, he knew he could only rely on himself.

Summoning all his strength once more, Detective Decker slowly rose from his seat and felt the warm gush of fresh blood flow. He knew the clock was ticking. He was thankful his body, though stiff, was in working order. He kept his hand on the bloody wound, applying as much direct pressure as he could muster, and fought the blackness creeping in on both sides of his vision.

Stumbling over to the small medical module, he removed a first aid kit, set it to one side, and unzipped the plastic bag. He removed surgical tape and some gauze pads. Feverishly, he tore open the packets, pressed wads of pads in place and quickly taped over the wound. Field dressing in place, he knew he had to get to the radio and call for help before any of the other mercenaries found him. The radio would be in the cockpit.

Decker noticed a soft glow emanating from the cockpit on the upper flight deck, and was drawn to the light. *Maybe the flight crew is still alive.* Navigating through the wrecked cargo bay area on shaky legs, he searched for Kate and checked for other survivors as he went. There was no sign of either, only more dead mercenaries.

Decker then remembered what was most likely the cause of the crash. Quickly scanning his surroundings, he didn't see any signs of the bear. Most likely it had fallen out of the helicopter or hadn't survived the crash, but Decker wasn't taking any chances. He grabbed a sidearm from one of the nearest of the dead commandos, a Glock 21. He press checked the slide and confirmed there was a round in the chamber. Decker knew from his previous encounter that the .45 caliber rounds would be little more than a deterrent for ol' Grumpy, but at least he had some sort of defense if any of the other commandos had survived the crash. He checked the dead commando's pouches, found two spare magazines, and slipped them both into his jacket pocket.

At least ol' Grumpy is nowhere to be found. So that's something.

As he got closer to the cockpit, the smell of burnt flesh became stronger. He unwrapped a musk-ox scarf from a mercenary who wore his head on backwards and used the fabric to cover his mouth and nose.

As he climbed up the short ladder that led up to the flight deck, Decker surveyed the cockpit and confirmed the worst. The windshield had collapsed. The pilots and the right side of the crumpled cockpit had fused into a mass of flesh and metal. Small fires consumed what was left of the bodies. His hopes diminished further when he noticed that the communications console was smashed and incapable of sending a signal. His only chance of rescue now was if the ELT had survived the crash and was generating a signal to allow rescuers to locate the crash site.

A freezing wind blew in from the ruptured windshield, making him shudder. As he rubbed his shoulders and stamped his feet for warmth, he noticed that he could see his own breath coming in small clouds.

Decker knew the first order of business was survival. *Better get moving, Decker, or you're gonna freeze to death for sure*, he told himself, and then mocking his old cantankerous survival instructor said aloud, "You can't help anybody if you're dead."

Wincing from the pain in his shoulder, Decker stifled a groan and climbed back down the ladder. He stopped in his tracks when he heard a deep guttural noise. It sounded like a grunt, like that of a large animal, coming from the payload area.

Oh, crap. Oh crap, oh crap, oh crap!

He found a flashlight in a receptacle near the bottom of the ladder, switched it on, and to his surprise, it still worked. He danced the beam across the remainder of the fuselage and heard the heavy grunt again.

C'mon, how much can one guy take?

Flashing his yellow beam about, he scanned the vast, dimly lit fuselage. He spied two four-wheel-drive Land Cruisers strapped to the deck. There was another body lying on the hood of one of them, half of a body anyway. The other half of the poor guy was probably amongst the miscellaneous cargo containers strewn about.

He strained his ears, listening for the grunting sound again, but could only hear the crackling fires behind him and howling wind assaulting the broken fuselage outside.

Well, Grumpy, I can't stay in here forever.

Decker was about to move deeper into the cavernous cargo hold, and continue his search for the ELT or a backup radio, when he heard another low guttural growl. Decker's eyes grew wide with surprise as a large furry mouth with gleaming white jaws came slowly, but purposefully, out of the shadows, to latch onto the body that was on the hood of the jeep and drag it off into the darkness.

Damn. Grumpy had survived the crash after all.

Decker lowered his firearm, knowing first-hand that the .45 caliber bullets would be of little use against the fearsome and desperate predator. He slowly backed away. Decker could hear Grumpy snacking on the hood ornament corpse and figured it was time to exit the transport.

He pushed away the awful thought of never seeing Kate again and focused back on the task of survival. At least he hadn't found her body yet, so that meant there was still a chance, however remote, that she was still alive.

His head began reeling and he reached out to the nearby cargo netting for support. When the netting turned in his hands, he saw a mangled body inside, presumably flung there during the crash. Decker quickly let go of the net and heard a maniacal cry escape his own lips. He buried his mouth in the back of his hand, not wanting to alert Grumpy to his presence.

It was time to venture outside.

After unfastening the locks of a nearby hatch, he tumbled through the hatchway into a fresh patch of snow. He checked behind him to make sure Grumpy wasn't following. Fortunately, no sign, and even if Grumpy did decide to leave the smorgasbord inside the chopper, Decker doubted the giant bear could fit his enormous girth through the small hatch opening.

The air was cool and the climate arid. The storm had either abated or they had flown farther south than he had imagined.

Body still stiff, wound aching, Decker drew himself up slowly. He resisted the urge to call out for Kate as he did not want to alert Grumpy or any other surviving commandos. Instead, he took in his immediate surroundings.

Stepping backwards, boots crunching in wet snow, he saw that the crumpled Chinook was now a sad relic of its former self, only one-fourth its original size. Smoke rose from the twisted and smoldering wreckage. The once proud twin rotor blades had either broken off or were bent into useless S-turns. Parachutes, cables, life jackets, cargo boxes, broken landing gear, and other fragments were littered everywhere in the slushy snow. It looked more like an aircraft junkyard spread out over the icy landscape than an aircraft.

Decker gazed at the trail of wreckage behind the big bird. He could only guess that it must have just cleared the nearby ridge before smashing down onto the ice like a lawn dart.

Worse still, the bent and broken fuselage rested on a glacier shelf of a frozen waterfall.

If the heat from the smoldering fires melts the ice, the helicopter's voyage might not be over.

As though the ice pack were reading his thoughts, Decker suddenly felt the ice rumble faintly beneath his insulated boots. Fortunately, the tremors ended as quickly as they had begun.

Decker glanced at his multi-sensor watch and saw the temperature reading displayed thirty degrees, just barely below freezing. But as the fires died out, it would get a lot colder. Another catch 22: if the fires didn't collapse the glacier under his feet, then he would freeze to death when they burned out.

Perfect.

Surveying the vast icefield that stretched out to every horizon, Decker was reminded of the fact that Alaska was a vast wild country two-and-a-half times the size of Texas, with a population of less than seven hundred thousand, and most of those lived in the safety and warmth of Anchorage and Fairbanks. This was a wilderness where humanity was not meant to tread. The wind stirred up the snow, flakes spitting into his face, and he was rudely brought back to his present predicament. *Think, Decker. We were heading south for at least thirty minutes, most likely towards Eielson Air Force Base. The CH-74 has a top speed of 196 miles per hour, which means we must be still somewhere in the Brooks Range.* Then Decker recognized the two large landmark mountains that flanked the North Fork Koyukuk River.

"The Arctic Gates," he breathed aloud. *Damn, we really are smack dab in the middle of nowhere.* Even if a rescue plane knew where to search for them, it would be nearly impossible to spot them amongst the hundred thousand glaciers that covered more than thirty thousand square miles of the Last Frontier.

The Aleuts had it right when they chose the name Alaska, the Great Country.

That was when he heard the scream.

That sounded like Kate!

Then he heard a man's voice say, "Shut up, will you just shut up?"

"You shut up," the woman shouted back.

Yep, that's Kate alright.

Chapter 34

Kate Hanging by a Thread

Like everyone else left alive in the crash, Kate had been knocked unconscious. When the gonging in her ears finally subsided, she heard a steady, howling wind. A sickening sensation in her stomach forced her to open her eyes. Beneath her dangling boots was a two-hundred-foot drop into open air. Kate tried to scream, but fear stole her breath. As she gasped, she became more aware of her surroundings. She found herself strapped into an airplane seat suspended by several straps of cargo netting, hanging off a glacial waterfall of luminous blue ice. She was too afraid to move her head; she wondered what held the straps above. She remembered traveling in the Chinook helicopter transport and looking out the window, the mountainous Arctic landscape passing steadily by. She remembered the big mercenary, Vlad, had taken Decker to the back of the plane. She wasn't quite sure what had happened next. It was all so hazy, fragmented. She did remember bringing the flute to her lips. Then … there was screaming. Lots of screaming. Amidst the chaos, Decker had somehow reappeared and shoved her into a seat and strapped her in. He had said something about the flight deck and then vanished. Shortly after that, the plane tilted crazily to one side, more cargo containers flew out the back and then …

Did we crash?

In any other situation, the expansive ice-covered valley around her would seem beautiful … were it not going to be her final resting place. Worst of all, she didn't even know if Decker had survived the crash.

No, Kate, you can't think like that. You've got to stay positive or you will never see Decker again.

"Help," Kate finally managed. She had intended a yell, but her voice was only a trembling whimper. Regardless, the blistering wind that froze the cheeks of her face was her only answer. A loud SNAP, and her seat dropped a few more inches. This time Kate did find her voice. She screamed as loud as a banshee.

As her scream was dying a slow, echoing death, she heard a man's voice snap. "Shut up, will you? Just shut up!" then muttering, "You'll cause a damn avalanche."

Given her spitfire nature, Kate answered automatically: "You shut up."

She twisted her head and risked a look overhead. She spied the Major, in his own seat about four feet above hers. Only a half-dozen taut straps separated them. They were about ten feet below the ridgeline. The cargo netting spilled over the cliff's edge, and she knew that the net was the only thing that had stopped their fatal descent.

"Hang on down there," the extremely large man with spiked hair shouted from above. Kate recognized him as Vlad. "I'll get a rope down to you."

"No time for that," the Major yelled back up to him. "Even if you find some rope you'll never get it down to us in time. You've got to pull us up by the netting *now!*"

There were a few seconds of tugging, followed by a series of popping noises, and Kate could see where the net had ripped in several places. The five or six straps above the Major were taut and looked as though they might give way at any second. The Major must've seen this too, for he shouted up to him, "Vlad! Stop it! The net's breaking!"

Vlad just looked down at them for a few moments that seemed endless. Then he finally said, "I'm not strong enough to pull you both up. You're too heavy together and the net's splitting. You've got to cut the woman loose."

"Are you insane?" Kate asked in disbelief.

But as much as she hated to admit it, Kate saw Vlad's logic. Above the Major, the cargo straps were beginning to fray.

This is insane!

As few as three days ago, she never would have imagined herself literally hanging by a thread over a bottomless chasm.

The Major's emotionless clear blue eyes staring down at her told her the truth. He didn't say anything. Still locking eyes with her, he simply unsheathed his jagged survival knife and began sawing away at the straps.

Chapter 35

Decker and Vlad

Boots crunching rapidly in the snow, Decker raced toward Kate's scream. He followed the trail of debris behind the crashed Chinook. Cargo netting sprouted from the rear of the wreckage and spread out on the ice like giant tail feathers, and the net continued outward until it spilled over the nearby cliff.

The small mountain of a man, Vlad, was lying on the cliff's edge, shouting to someone below. Hearing Decker's approach, the highly trained mercenary rolled to his feet and grabbed for his rifle.

Decker fumbled in his parka for his Glock.

Instead of shooting him, Vlad shot out a front thrust kick to Decker's chest and knocked him down.

Head swimming in stars from where it had bounced off the ice, Decker managed to sit up. Vlad towered over him.

"Oh, good. You survived too," Decker grumbled irritably, now on his backside in the snow. Decker casually reached for his sidearm, but realized he must have dropped it in the snow. Spying it a few feet away, he was about to make a desperate lunge for it when he heard the distinct sound of an M-16 chambering a round.

"I wouldn't if I were you," Vlad said venomously. "The only reason I didn't kill you is I need your help pulling the Major back up to the surface."

That said, Vlad stretched out a hand the size of a catcher's mitt, grabbed Decker by the coat, and yanked him swiftly to his feet.

Wincing from the pain in his shoulder, he asked, "Well, Mr. Vlad, any idea where we went down?"

Before the big merc could answer, a voice boomed in the distance. "Vlad, get your ass back over here and pull me up!"

Hearing this, Vlad turned back towards him and responded, "No time for that, the straps are breaking loose!"

Decker shook his head in confusion. "What are you talking about, what straps?"

Instead of answering, the big man grabbed him roughly by the shoulder and shoved him towards the ledge.

Careful of his proximity to the frozen waterfall's edge and to the big merc behind him with the rifle, Decker moved closer and peered over the cliff's side. He saw two people dangling off the cliff, still belted into their seats. They were about ten feet below the ridgeline. Miraculously, the cargo net had stopped their fatal descent.

Oh my God, one of them is Kate!

Thinking quickly, he told Vlad, "Listen, I saw a rope and harness in the duty locker. We could lower it down to them and haul them up one at a time."

"No time for that," Vlad spat back. "Even if you find rope, you'll never get it down to them before they fall."

Decker didn't think the net could take much more, but he grabbed hold of the net and both men began to tug.

A few straps snapped and Vlad snapped through clenched teeth, "The two of them are too heavy for the net to hold if we pull them up together."

"Try harder," Decker grunted as he pulled.

"Stop, stop," the Major demanded. "You keep pulling and you're just going to sever the net on the ice."

Decker could hear Kate sobbing now.

"They're just too heavy together." Vlad gasped. Catching his breath, he leaned back over the edge and shouted, "Major, listen to me. There's just no other way. You're going to have to cut the woman loose."

"What?" Decker asked in disbelief. He practically lunged over the edge and shouted down to the Major, "Don't you even think about cutting her loose, Major." He glanced back at the wreckage, an idea forming, and then shouted back down to them, "Just hold on for a few minutes longer. I've got an idea."

To Vlad, Decker shouted, "I'm going for the rope and harness." He then shouted back down over the edge, "Kate, hang on down there! I'm getting some rope."

But Decker could see the Major was already sawing away at the net.

Chapter 36

Severed

"Don't you do it. Don't you cut that net," Kate heard Decker's voice say once he returned. She could barely make him out up on the ledge. At the moment, he was uncoiling a rope. It was a sweet gesture, but the stressed fabric of the net and the psychotic glaze in the Major's eyes told her that Decker's rope would never reach her in time. A few more straps snapped above the Major. All this struggling didn't matter. Not anymore. In another moment, they'd both fall to their deaths anyway.

The Major also noted the snapping fibers above him. "I'm so sorry, Dr. Foster," he said. "I had hoped to deliver you to Grondal alive, but as the French say, 'C'est la vie'."

Kate understood why the Major had to do it, but it didn't stop her from hating him for it.

Her eyes darted around for any possible means of escape. She was dangling too far away from the frozen waterfall, and even if she could reach it, Kate knew she'd never get a toehold in the ice wall. Her only choice was to climb up over the Major and scramble the rest of the way up the net. But first, she would have to get out of her seat. Most likely she would fall the moment she released her seatbelt, but she had to try. She reached up, wound the net around her left arm, and clung fiercely to it. She then reached down to unbuckle her seat with her free hand.

The Major must've spied what she was doing because she heard him say, "Kate, what the hell do you think you're doing?" She didn't answer. Instead, she pulled the release mechanism.

Kate tried to scream as her seat dropped away, but fear took her breath. She was hanging too far away from the ice wall to get a foothold and spun lazily around in circles.

Breathe, Kate. You've got to breathe.

Somehow she regained enough of her composure to suck in a little air and maintain it. "I can't hold on," she managed weakly.

"Nice try, Kate," the Major intoned. "I admire your tenacity, and I am truly sorry." But the Major wasn't waiting around for her to get tired and let go. He started in on the last of the net straps once more with his knife.

In that last brief moment, Kate accepted her fate. She didn't have the strength to climb up the net like she had planned, but she was damned if her last view on earth was going to be the Major's maniacal face telling her how sorry he was for murdering her.

Instead, she gazed at the ice enshrouded valley below. Beautiful. Majestic. It would make a nice little resting place .... At least she could die knowing her theories were proven right. Even if the rest of the world would never know it.

She closed her eyes. The only sounds were the sawing of the knife, the wind whistling across the ice, ... and finally her own heartbeat, thundering in her ears. She heard the last of the net fibers giving way, and when the final SNAP came, her eyes shot open. There was a sickening moment of freefall as her body began to plunge toward the vast chasm below. She figured that rescuers probably wouldn't even be able to recover her smashed up body.

If only I had gotten to see him one last time.

All those thoughts passed in that brief millisecond as she fell, her eyes wide open.

Thinking it her imagination, she thought she glimpsed Decker running sideways alongside the mountain, which was ludicrous, of course. She could hear his rapid footfalls on the ice as he sprinted madly towards her in a dance that defied gravity. Crazily, she thought, *how the hell is he doing that,* but she knew instinctively he would never reach her in time.

That's when she heard Decker say, "Gotcha." She felt a pair of strong arms encircling her; they were so tight she couldn't breathe. She didn't care because she wasn't falling anymore.

It was Decker with the rope. He must have rapelled down to her level, run towards her on the cliff wall of ice, and caught her the moment the Major had severed the net.

Still holding her, Decker asked her quietly, "You okay?" Somehow he had wrapped his line around her and was holding them both effortlessly now. He needn't have bothered; her fingers dug so deeply into his jacket that he didn't have to support her.

"Aww, isn't that sweet," the Major said sarcastically. Then, turning his head towards the surface he shouted upwards, "Vlad, shoot them. Shoot them both."

"Copy that," Vlad said efficiently down to them. He maneuvered his rifle over the edge and took aim at them.

Decker had only time to gaze in her eyes one last time and say, "Sorry, Kate, I tried."

Kate nodded her head repeatedly at him, tears streaming down her cheeks. "If only we had more time." With nothing else they could do, they pressed their foreheads together and waited for the inevitable sniper shots to ring out.

—— <> ——

On the ledge above them, Vlad calmly and methodically adjusted his scope. He knew he could've just as easily severed Decker's rope, but this was way more fun and he'd have a great story to tell his pals back home. He set the crosshairs on the detective and whispered, "Sorry, but the plucky American hero doesn't get to win this tale."

Vlad's concentration was so focused on his target that he didn't even feel the jagged teeth slip over his ankle until they bit down and yanked him backwards.

Vlad screamed and started kicking with his free leg frantically. It didn't matter. Teeth sheared through his flesh and crushed the bone.

Still holding him by the ankle, the monstrosity shook him like a favorite chew toy. When the bear finally let go, Vlad flew through the air and landed on a rock ten feet away.

He felt like he had been struck by a bus. The bear's single blow had inflicted severe damage, including the loss of Vlad's right eye, nose, and right side of his scalp.

Lying in a crumpled heap, face pressed to the ice, he tried to draw up enough strength to crawl away. Before he could, his leg was suddenly snagged up by his heel again in that same painful vice-like grip. He was lifted upside down and held there as if he weighed no more than a feather. Aware of his own imminent death, Vlad had an upside-down view of the crumpled Chinook.

The bear shook him several more times before dropping him roughly to the ground. Sobbing, a wave of nausea swept over him. He was in excruciating pain. Vlad felt like a pile of broken and mutilated human garbage, but he was still alive. Disoriented, he heard his breath come in thin whistles.

Did I puncture a lung?

The attack was over as quickly as it had begun. He could no longer sense the bear's presence, nor could he see him out of his remaining eye. He had read once that bears attack their victims and then leave them for dead. He could only pray that was the case now. Reaching blindly to wipe the blood from the left side of his face, he felt a thin slippery mass and, with horror, he realized he was holding the stem of his own dislodged eye.

He became dimly aware of a loud snorting breath.

Just play dead, Vlad, and you might survive this yet.

The ground shook beneath his cheek and Vlad knew the bear was circling him. Despite the pain, he forced open his one good remaining eye and glimpsed an enormous paw as it padded past his ruined face.

C'mon, I'm dead, leave me alone already, he screamed internally.

Just when he thought the pain couldn't possibly be any worse, he felt jaws slip over either side of his face. The last thing Vlad heard was teeth grating on his skull and the bones in his jaw cracking as the bear started chewing on his head.

—— <> ——

Down below, foreheads still pressed together, waiting for their imminent execution, Decker looked up when he heard

Vlad's scream. He thought he glimpsed the big mercenary get violently pulled back from the edge.

When they heard the bear roar, Vlad's demise was immediately apparent.

"You've got to be kidding me!" Major Barauch roared. Then seeing Decker and Kate were staring at him he said, "Well, you want a job done right ..." Barauch kicked so he was over top of them and was trying to grab their rope.

Unarmed, Decker was trying to think of options.

"He's got the rope," Kate yelled.

Decker's leg kicked the cargo netting hanging beneath the Major. He quickly grabbed hold of it and pulled.

Above them, the Major held their rope in one hand and his knife next to it in another. "Good-bye, Detective..." he began to say, but then yelped in surprise when Decker yanked on the cargo netting. There was a loud series of POPS as the frayed netting snapped in quick succession. But the Major only dropped a few feet, releasing the knife as he did; it went tumbling past Kate's ear.

"Stop!" the Major yelled. "What are you doing?"

Decker stared up at the Major one last time, and without taking his eyes off him, gave one last good yank.

The Major screamed as he flew by them. Kate was afraid the Major was going to grab at them as he sailed past, but he was too quickly out of reach.

The Major's scream hadn't even finished echoing off the glacial walls when a second noise replaced them.

A bright red helicopter rose up in front of them. At first Kate thought it was more mercenaries, but through the window, she saw Vickers's spiky blonde hair.

"Now, how did they find us?" Decker asked.

Kate unzipped her coat pocket and pulled out a device that looked like a capsule. "Probably with this." When Decker stared at her questioningly she said, "Vickers gave it to me before we left. She said it was a precaution."

Through an external loudspeaker, Vickers's voice said, "Dex, we're going to land, and then pull you up."

Decker flashed her the thumbs-up sign, and the helicopter rose to the surface.

After landing on the ledge, rescue workers piled out and yelled down to them to hang on because they were going to pull them to safety. Decker immediately yelled back to the rescue team and alerted them about the bear. Vickers nodded in understanding, but thus far there was no sign of him.

Satisfied he'd done what he could to warn the rescue team, Decker looked away from the workers up top and gazed into her eyes. "Hey, what do you say we get out of here?"

It was slow going, but soon they were back up on the ledge. As Kate came over the ledge, she barely recognized the crumpled Chinook behind the rescue helicopter. She could not even begin to count how many times she had cheated death in the last twenty-four hours.

Vickers came running towards her. "Oh, thank God! We thought we lost you two."

Kate returned Vickers's hug and then heard a KA-CHINK behind her. Kate turned. Decker had loosened the straps of his harness and dropped it to the ground so he could step out of it.

Kate saw Vickers walk over to him. "Dex, I have to admit, that was pretty awesome." But then her expression changed to a more serious tone and told him, "Uh, Dex, your shoulder, it's bleeding pretty bad."

Vickers was right. Kate saw the entire right side of Decker's clothes was soaked in blood. It appeared as though the blood was seeping from a shoulder wound he must've sustained in the crash.

"What? This? This is nothing." But before anyone could catch him, Decker fell over into the snow.

Vickers and Kate reached him at the same time. They gently maneuvered him onto his back. As Decker lay there with his head in Kate's lap, she wiped the snow from his face.

Decker fought hard to stay conscious. He smiled up at her and barely managed to tell her, "Kate. You're safe now. You tell the world what you found."

"Don't talk," Kate told him, tears streaming off her face and landing on his.

"I need medics over here!" Vickers shouted, but the light began to fade from Decker's eyes.

Kate had wanted to thank him for saving her life, but it was too late. He was already gone.

Epilogue

Five Days Later

Kate's rescue from the ice waterfall had unfolded without any further drama.

As Vickers had promised, the transport had gotten Decker to the Fairbanks Emergency Medical in record time. He had had to be resuscitated twice in midflight, but after the third attempt he had managed to hang on for the duration.

During the first week, every doctor attending him had told Kate how lucky he was to still be above ground after losing so much blood.

Vickers had hovered around until she was assured by the medical staff that he was on the mend. Satisfied with his status, she had flown down to Anchorage for additional debriefing. Thus far, the mercenaries that they had encountered had been identified as exactly that. Unfortunately, nothing, electronic or otherwise, nothing but Kate's unsubstantiated testimony, had been found to tie them to the president of Iceland.

Peeking in on him, Kate saw that Decker's daughter was still curled up in the hospital bed beside him. She had refused to leave his side since she had been flown in, and a small bed littered with stuffies and dolls lay next to Decker's bed.

"I love you, Daddy."

"I love you more, baby-girl," Decker answered through half-slit eyes.

"Sam's still asleep in the cafeteria with Grandma, but there is someone else who is waiting to see you," Alexandria said, smiling devilishly.

"And who might that be?" Decker asked, his eyebrows raised in mock innocence.

"It's a girl," Alex said, singing the word girl. "She's been waiting for you to wake up for like, ever."

Decker spied Kate at the door. "Why don't you send her in and go check on your little brother."

"Okay, daddy." Little Alex hugged him hard. James groaned in pain, but still managed to keep smiling.

"Bye Daddy," then to her, "Bye Miss Kate."

"See ya later, alligator," Kate immediately responded.

"After awhile, crocodile," Alexandria shot back.

"See you soon, baboon."

From down the hall, Alexandria shouted, "Getting wise, bubble-eyes."

It was a game they had played often during those first few days while waiting for him to wake up.

Kate sat down on the bed beside him and handed him the cup of Americano she had bought at the popular coffee chain across the street. After checking warily for one of the many nurses who always seemed to be at his bedside in abundance, he sipped at it greedily.

"How are you feeling today, Detective?"

Decker managed a lopsided grin between sips. "Probably about as bad as I look."

"Wow, that bad, huh?"

Decker smiled up at her. "Dr. Foster, was that a joke?"

Kate shrugged her shoulders. "If you have to ask, probably not a very good one."

"Don't worry, according to my kids, it's nothing a few weeks at Disney World won't cure."

Kate shook her head in disbelief, and said, smiling through her tears, "You're hopeless."

"That's how I roll."

They laughed for a few moments longer. Then there was an awkward silence before Kate managed, "How much do you know?"

James sighed. "Everything's still pretty hazy after the crash. Vickers walked me through most of it. I remember her telling me all the mercs are dead. After the rescue team returned to the crash site, they found the jade totem missing and assumed it got sucked out of the plane." When he saw her drop her gaze down to the floor he added, "Sorry, Kate."

"I think that's the worst part. All of my friends died, and we've got nothing to show for it other than Eugene's flute."

"Where's it now?"

This brought a small smile to Kate's lips. "The real one is back down in Anchorage, at the university." Kate drew what appeared to be the flute from beneath her shirt. "A colleague of mine made a 3-D printer copy of it and gave this to me at the funeral." She played a few small sad notes, but it was clear she had been practicing. "Sounds identical to the original."

"That's great, Kate," Decker said. "You guys ever figure out how it controlled the bear?"

"Just theories, really. The most ludicrous one is that the prehistoric bear was thawed out of the ice and woke up after a ten-thousand-year nap."

"But you don't believe that?"

Kate shook her head. "I do believe that a pre-Neolithic culture domesticated the bears for thousands of years before the last Ice Age, yes, but what I think is more likely is these bears flourished in the remote areas of the Arctic and retained the genetic trait to obey the flute."

Decker winced as he attempted to sit up, but then decided against it. "That must've been some city, right? I mean, can you imagine what it must've been like? Those giant bears, and who knows what else, co-existing with a race of ancient people?"

Kate nodded, glancing toward the blinds, and her expression quickly hardened. "What bothers me the most is that murderous bastard, Grondal, just gets away with it. Vickers searched for the mercs' laptop, but they couldn't find it or any evidence of any kind linking those mercenaries to him. She believes someone arrived after the rescue team left and cleaned the site of all evidence."

Decker thought about asking why no one had stayed behind to guard the site until the Bureau or army showed up, but he knew it would've been suicide for anybody to stay behind with that bear and maybe more mercs on the loose.

"I've been thinking about that too. I can't shake the feeling that there's a lot more here to this story than we think. The tip of the iceberg, as it were."

She was about to lose it, but James pulled her close and whispered, "Don't worry Kate, we'll get him." And for a time, they just stayed like that, foreheads together.

Finally, it was Decker who spoke first. "My head's still pretty rattled, but I think I remember you mentioned a second antechamber?"

Kate thought about her dropped flashlight, the light revealing marble stairs as it descended into icy depths. "Yes, only now it's buried under tons of rock and ice." Kate wiped away a tear from her cheek. "There's absolutely nothing we can do."

James said smiling, "Sure there is." When she stared at him expectantly he added, "Start digging."

Kate grabbed a nearby pillow and hit him with it.

"Man down, man down," Decker groaned.

Careful of his injuries, she lifted his bedsheet, crawled into his bed and lay down beside him. She was amazed how perfectly she fit next to him, like two pieces of a puzzle.

He stroked her hair for a time and kissed her temple. When he finally did speak again, his tone was filled with, for lack of a better word, wonder. She recalled how cynical he had been when they had first met. Clearly their experience in the Arctic had brought some lost childhood magic back to him. "You did it, Kate. You proved there are still some pretty amazing wonders left in the world to discover."

Instead of arguing, she just snuggled a little closer to him.

Her cell phone buzzed on the night table where she had left it. "I thought I turned that darn thing off." She was about to end the call and send it to voicemail when she saw that the caller was Vickers, so she answered it instead.

"Who is it?" Decker asked.

Instead of answering him she cheerfully said into her phone, "Hi Vick, guess who decided to stay awake ..." she began.

Vickers cut her off almost immediately. "You need to turn on the TV."

"What?" Kate asked, struck a little dumbfounded by Vickers's curt tone.

"You need to turn on the television, right now."

As Kate reached for the remote she asked, "Which channel?"

"Doesn't matter. I've got to go. I'll call you back when I can."

Decker raised his eyebrows and began to ask, but she pointed to the television.

The image on the television screen snapped on and showed a news camera pointing out the window of a hovering helicopter. The caption at the bottom of the screen read ...

12 CONFIRMED DEAD/16 STILL MISSING ON IDITAROD TRAIL

And changed to ...

ALYSSA BRYANT REPORTING LIVE FROM THE SCENE!

The scene below was of mass confusion. A rescue helicopter was hovering over a tiny ghost town of a village that was still smoldering in places. Several Alaska State Troopers SUVs and Fire Units were scattered about the ramshackle of a broken town like toy cars.

"Turn it up," Decker breathed, even as she was doing so.

The reporter's voice, wavering and barely keeping it together, was in mid-sentence as the television's volume rose. "Thus far, there have been no other survivors found and dozens of eyewitnesses reported seeing, and I quote, 'A giant grey bear, much too large for a polar bear'."

Kate was having trouble hearing the reporter's voice over the background noise from the helicopter's engine and rotors so she turned the volume up a bit louder. Decker remained speechless.

"All volunteers, mushers, and non-essential personnel have been evacuated from the Iditarod checkpoint of Takotna."

The hovering rescue helicopter changed its position slightly, and viewers could now see a victim being lifted up in a bright orange basket. The young female reporter must have seen this too for she announced, "Wait, it appears as though one survivor has been found and is being airlifted into a rescue helicopter." Another pause, and ... "Yes, I'm being told one survivor has been found, is in critical condition, and most likely will be medevac'd to Fairbanks Regional Hospital."

The onsite reporting was replaced by two news anchors behind their desk in the studio, one middle-aged male with greying hair and the other a smartly-dressed blonde-haired waif.

The male anchor was the first to compose himself. "For those of you just tuning in ... the Iditarod race has suffered a major catastrophe. Dozens have been killed and more are missing. Our onsite reporter Alyssa Bryant is reporting live to you from the scene as it unfolds."

Auditory exclusion. Kate was pretty sure that's what the experts called it. When the mind feels like it's slowing down, and one experiences temporary hearing loss due to high stress.

The hospital room vanished. Only the television set remained in a world of pitch blackness. Even now, the television was moving farther and farther away from her as its images flashed back and forth between the news anchors and the onsite reporter that she could no longer hear.

The world tilted a little crazily and the last thing she heard before even the television vanished completely was one worried cry from Decker.

"Kate?"

—— <> ——

Afterword

Note: Many of the bear attacks in the book were based on actual experiences and/or reports of encounters that I had collected while traveling all over Alaska.

My last job in the Arctic was protecting engineers from ravenous polar bears. As luck would have it, my first day on the job was easily the most dangerous, (and memorable). My partner had dropped me off at a remote checkpoint and was going back to the main camp to retrieve his forgotten lunch.

Not five minutes after his departure, a six-hundred-pound Mama polar bear and her only remaining cub climbed out of the Arctic Ocean and began loping in my direction. As I had just arrived to the Arctic, I only had my sidearm, (a .40 caliber Glock, which isn't nearly enough to slow down a normal-sized bear, let alone a much larger charging polar bear), and I had not yet been issued my duty shotgun.

When I radioed for help, the Sergeant told me to hide in the checkpoint, lock the door, and wait until backup arrived. Sizing up the flimsy guard shack, I radioed back, (a little grumpily), "Are you kidding me? That thing isn't going to keep me safe; I might as well be a snack pack."

Note: This was a nickname I did not enjoy for the next several days.

Since the polar bear was still a little ways off, I took out my camera and took as many pictures as I dared. Certain I had gotten some good photos, I drew my weapon and, if absolutely necessary, prepared to fire every last round into the charging bear. I was determined that, at the very least, they'd find left behind an empty magazine and some pretty cool pictures of a charging polar bear.

Sidebar: Now before I get any hate mail, I consider polar bears to be incredibly beautiful creatures and I would never consider harming one under any other condition than saving a human life.

To give you an idea of what it feels like to face down a charging polar bear, think of a car, (say the size of a VW bug), but it's not a car, it's a bear, with lots of teeth, and it's coming right at you to kill you, and eat you, and maybe not necessarily in that order. Because the first thing you learn in Arctic survival training is that to a polar bear, everything on the ice that moves is considered food, including you.

In the end, I would've been a "snack pack" if another patrol officer hadn't heard my radio calls for assistance and returned with a two-ton patrol vehicle with lights ablaze and siren blaring, scaring the magnificent creature, and her cub, away.

A Word On Detective Vickers

In the novel, the character Vickers wears many hats; she is a behavioral signals expert, a detective for the Alaska Bureau of Investigations, a bush pilot, an EMT II, and a survival instructor. Some might find it unbelievable that one person could possess all these skills. To this I offer the following:

Working with the Anchorage Police Department, Joint Terrorist Task Force, and high profile security, I was privileged to work with many professionals in the Last Frontier. It was not uncommon for law enforcement officers working in the bush to have all of these certifications and much more. In fact, many lives often depended on it.

I hope you have enjoyed *WHITE DEATH*. If you'd like a sneak peek at one of my other novels, you merely have to turn the page. You can also check out other real-life adventure stories and other upcoming novels on my website: www.JackCastlebooks.com

Until our paths cross again, dear reader,

— *Jack Castle*

If you enjoyed this read

Please leave a review on Amazon, Facebook, Good Reads or Instagram.

It takes less than five minutes and it really does make a difference.

If you're not sure how to leave a review on Amazon:

1. *Go to amazon.com.*

2. *Type in White Death by Jack Castle and when you see it, click on it.*

3. *Scroll down to Customer Reviews, nearby you'll see a box labeled Write a Review. Click it.*

4. *Now, if you've never written a review before on Amazon, they might ask you to create a name for yourself.*

5. *Reviews can be as simple as, "Loved the book! Can't wait for the Next!" (Please don't give the story away.)*

And that's it!

Brian Hades, publisher

Here's a sneak peek of other novels by real life adventurer, Jack Castle.

———< >———

Bedlam Lost

by Jack Castle

HavenPort: Population 492. A town with no roads in or out.

Deputy Hank McCarthy has just moved his family into the remote Alaskan town to replace the local Sheriff. He doesn't think a small sleepy town like HavenPort will offer much in the way of excitement but, considering what he's running from, he's more than happy about that.

New York City ballet dancer Emma Hudson is running from something too. Unlike Hank, she's not sure what she'll find in HavenPort, especially when supernatural terrors begin to haunt her dreams, and sometimes her waking hours. The people of HavenPort claim it's no cause for concern. No need to act crazy. She knows what crazy is like.

When Hank and Emma share a daytime terror they begin to see there's more to this town than they know. Unfortunately for them it's already too late. Their paths are chosen. There's no way out of HavenPort.

A supernatural sci-fi thriller, Bedlam Lost delivers for fans of Dean Koontz and J. J. Abrams' LOST. Step into this story and you might not be able to leave.

Praise for Bedlam Lost

"Bedlam. Just the name itself is chilling. But "chilling" hardly scratches the surface of the true atmosphere of this gripping story. It is startling at the on-set, gut-wrenching in it's horror, mind-boggling in it's unfolding terror. This book had my hands physically shaking. The characters draw you into their stories and you realize you are completely lost in the same confusion and fear they are experiencing. The best part? By the end, I could hardly differentiate what was reality from what was merely some thrilling fiction. To me, that in itself makes Bedlam a must read for all thrill seekers. But only if you think you're ready for the unguessable...."
— Hadassah Carter

"Just when you think everything has been said or done, along comes Bedlam Lost. Horror, sci-fi, mystery, suspense, and lots of action, this book kept me guessing right to the end! And WOW, I would never have expected that ending. DO NOT LET ANYONE TELL YOU THE ENDING!"
— Dennis Bryant

"Bedlam Lost raised the hair on the back of my neck right from the start. There were times when I thought it was okay to relax but I quickly realized that there is an element of terror around every corner. The story is intricate and fast-paced and the characters are well thought out. As terrifying as it was to read I enjoyed every minute of Bedlam Lost."
— Sarah Jameson

For more on Bedlam Lost visit:
tinyurl.com/edge6008

—— <> ——

Europa Journal

By Jack Castle

The history of humanity is about to change forever...

On 5 December 1945, five TBM Avenger bombers embarked on a training mission off the coast of Florida and mysteriously vanish without a trace in the Bermuda Triangle. A PBY search and rescue plane with thirteen crewmen aboard sets out to find the Avengers . . . and never returns.

In 2168, a mysterious five-sided pyramid is discovered on the ocean floor of Jupiter's icy moon, Europa.

Commander Mac O'Bryant and her team of astronauts are among the first to enter the pyramid's central chamber. They find the body of a missing World War II pilot, whose hands clutch a journal detailing what happened to him after he and his crew were abducted by aliens and taken to a place with no recognizable stars. As the pyramid walls begin to collapse around Mac and her team, their names mysteriously appear within its pages and they find themselves lost on an alien world.

Stranded with no way home, Mac decides to retrace the pilot's steps. She never expects to find the man alive. And if the man has yet to die, what does that mean for her and the rest of her crew?

Praise for Europa Journal

This book kept me guessing! It has an exciting start and keeps that same pace throughout the book. The building of

the character personalities keeps a depth to the storyline and makes the reader feel connected to each character. The background information given through Europa Journal gives a great balance between the history, future and everything in-between! I love the mix of fact and fiction to create the story and inspire imagination. I'm excited to see what Castle comes up with next!
— Dianna Temple

With an action-packed opening, page-turning twists,a well-built world, and characters worth caring about, Europa Journal is like a bulldog - it grabbed me and wouldn't let go! It seamlessly blends breathtaking imagination with the gritty reality of survival, and beautifully blurs what has been with what might be. I love Dr. Who and grew up with Star Trek, but this book has broken the sci-fi mold in a wonderful way!
— Stuntwoman, Elisa Brinton

From the opening space shuttle crash landing to the stunning finish, Europa Journal is a real page turner. Ancient astronauts, the Bermuda triangle, WW II pilots, space shuttle crews – what else could you ask for? Mr. Castle keeps the story at light speed, with plenty of twists and turns before the awesome climax!
— James Wahlman, Firefighter in Alaska

For more on Europa Journal visit:
tinyurl.com/edge6001

For more Science Fiction, Fantasy, and Speculative Fiction titles from EDGE and EDGE-Lite visit us at:

www.edgewebsite.com

Don't forget to sign-up for our Special Offers

JACK CASTLE

Author Biography

Jack Castle loves adventure. He has traveled the globe as a professional stuntman for stage, film, and television. While working for Universal Studios, he met Cinderella at Walt Disney World and they were soon married. After moving to Alaska, he worked as a tour guide, police officer, Criminal Justice professor, and certified weapons instructor. He has been stationed on a remote island in the Aleutians as a Response Team Commander and his last job in the Arctic Circle was protecting engineers from ravenous polar bears. He has had several Alaska adventure stories published along with articles in international security periodicals and he has written three novels: Europa Journal, Bedlam Lost, and White Death.

For more real life adventures with Jack Castle
or information on his upcoming books
check out his web page at:

http://www.jackcastlebooks.com/

Made in United States
North Haven, CT
11 March 2024

49851563R00134